QUEEROES 2

STEVEN BEREZNAI

Queeroes 2

Third edition

Copyright © 2013, 2018, 2021 Steven Bereznai

Jambor Publishing

Cover by Demented Doctor Design

ISBN 978-1-989055-07-6 (print)

ISBN 978-1-989055-08-3(ebook)

Names: Bereznai, Steven, author.

Title: Queeroes 2 / Steven Bereznai.

Description: Third edition. | Toronto : Jambor Publishing, [2021]

Identifiers: ISBN: 978-1-989055-07-6 (print) | 978-1-989055-08-3 (ebook)

Subjects: LCSH: Young gay men--Fiction. | Lesbian youth--Fiction. | Gay teenagers--Fiction. | Superheroes--Fiction. | Supervillains--Fiction. | High school students--Fiction. | High school athletes--Fiction. | Cheerleaders--Fiction. | Good and evil--Fiction. | Young adult fiction. | GSAFD: Fantasy fiction. | LCGFT: Bildungsromans. | Science fiction. | Action and adventure fiction. | Romance fiction.

Classification: LCC: PR9199.4.B4695 Q442 2021 | PS8553.E6358 | DDC: 813/.6--dc23

For Michael.
You have the keenest of insights,
The sharpest of wits,
And the warmest of hearts.
I'm honored and humbled to have you on my side.

Previously, on QUEEROES...

After drinking bottles of Etienne water contaminated with an experimental isotope, a group of teens in the small town of Nuffim developed incredible powers. It only affected gay guys and straight women in their adolescent years—for science reasons.

Emotionally repressed and closeted jock Troy Allstar became an empath, able to sense and control people's feelings; his scrawny, nerdy brother Gibbie grew super strong; attention-seeking cheerleader Mandy developed the ability to turn invisible and create a forcefield; her bestie, sassy but insecure cheerleader Chad, faced his daddy issues and unleashed his inner animal.

Working together, they defeated a pair of super-powered classmates out to destroy the school. The Queeroes now face a new threat—a mysterious note written in the journal Chad gave his beau Troy:

They know who you are, and they know what you can do. They came for us, now they're coming for you.

Nothing behind me, everything ahead of me, as is ever so on the road.

—Jack Kerouac, *On the Road*

Chapter 1

Take me home...

The words from the Guns N' Roses song swirled through nineteen-year-old Jake Kanaan's brain as his fingers twitched on the steering wheel of his jeep. The lyrics made his spirit itch, eager to belt off a few riffs on his electric guitar. Too bad he'd hocked the instrument along with most of his worldly goods.

He sighed and stared down a dirt road hemmed by forest on either side, dappled sunbeams poking through the evergreens. His dented jeep idled, belching fumes. Jake shifted in his seat, torn vinyl digging into his backside.

What am I doing here? he wondered.

He tapped his thumbs to a tune he'd been working on, playing with lyrics inspired by Kerouac. Jake was aiming for 'Once In a Lifetime,' but everything came out 'Jagged Little Pill.'

"Drama queen," he muttered to himself. The femme/fun phrase tasted foreign in his masc/musc mouth; it also contrasted with his look—porn star meets rock god. His faded GNR T-shirt hugged his muscular frame, the fabric worn thin as it stretched across the mounds of his chest and biceps. He'd lost his football scholarship and was booted from the team after missing too many practices, but his bod (and cheekbones) remained trophy-worthy. His naturally brown skin was bronzed even deeper from working shirtless at random construction gigs, and he liked to mess with his model looks; his tousled hair was shaved on the sides; a faux diamond glittered from each ear; a tattoo of colorful orchids covered his right arm.

His genes were made for haute couture, but his ripped denim bellowed delinquent.

None of that stopped his pulse from racing as he stared down a not-so-yellow brick road lined with poison ivy, leading to the most infamous brotherhood *not* allowed to be part of the nearby university campus.

Rockman Hall—the new, unsanctioned, gay fraternity. *Gayternity*, the school rag called it, officially banned because it "discriminated" based on sexual orientation—not because the provost was a raging homophobe. Jake's booted foot pressed gently on the accelerator, and the jeep crunched toward an old country house with a wraparound deck in need of a fresh coat of paint. He stopped the jeep next to three other vehicles—a Porsche, a battered black van, and a sleek BMW motorbike.

I can't believe I'm thinking of joining. What if they hit on me? he wondered, followed by, *What if they don't?*

He looked over his shoulder. It would be so easy to take off.

OFFER THEM WHAT THEY SECRETLY WANT AND THEY OF COURSE IMMEDIATELY BECOME PANIC-STRICKEN, a deep male voice startled him. Jake looked around, but no one was there. He recognized the Kerouac quote; it had been haunting him for months.

"Now, I'm hearing things. Crazy," Jake said.

THE ONLY PEOPLE FOR ME ARE THE MAD ONES, THE ONES WHO ARE MAD TO LIVE, MAD TO TALK, MAD TO BE SAVED, the voice said again.

More Kerouac. It was like the speaker was there, but not. Jake turned off the ignition. More and more, it seemed like the voice was talking from inside his head. He'd been spending a lot of time on his own, on the road, in his tent, in no-name peeler bars where his worth was measured in crumpled dollar bills. No wonder he was losing it.

"Here goes," he sighed.

He mirror-checked his wavy hair, got out, and slammed the jeep door behind him. He bounded athletically up the front steps and tried lifting the metal handle of a rusted door knocker. It wouldn't move. He looked closer; it was melted and mangled. To his left, a handprint seemed to be burned into the door frame.

"What the eff?" he swore.

"Are you going to stand there all day or are you going to come in?" someone said from behind him.

It sounded like the voice that had been in his head. This time, it wasn't his imagination. He stared into the beautiful brown eyes of one of the most handsome young men he'd ever seen, leaning out the front window. The guy looked like a jacked Lenny Kravitz.

"I'm Felix. We spoke on the phone."

"Yeah," Jake said, "I recognize the voice."

"I've been known to get inside people's heads," Felix smiled. "Don't tell my boyfriend. He's scary when he's jealous."

"I know the type," Jake replied. His heart trembled, memories freezing his feet to the doormat.

Felix nodded sympathetically.

"It's hard to go after what you want when you're worrying about something, or someone, you've left behind. That's why so many people wind up standing still."

Or running away, Jake thought.

Felix nodded. "That's what I love about this place. Every time I walk through the door, it feels like I'm home. Come in. Everyone's psyched to meet the new pledge."

"If I decide to join," Jake said.

"If you pass the hazing," Felix winked, opening the door and guiding Jake into the front hall.

A shiny plaque above the door made Jake's brow furrow.

Enter to serve, go forth to rule, he read.

"We're still debating that motto," Felix admitted.

"Speak for yourself," a young man said as he descended the staircase. He had sharp features, jet black hair swooped back and ending in shiny curls, and a build that curved just right in his blue Armani jacket. A yellow Prada button-down with a crisp collar and diamond-studded cufflinks poked out. "Someone has to lead *and* reap the benefits. Is it our fault we've been chosen? Hola, I'm Alejandro." He was the 5th Avenue Latinx version of Felix, handsome and muscled in his form-fitting ensemble.

"The earrings are an interesting choice," Alejandro said, his palm warm in Jake's hand. "But we're not in Jersey." His fingers slipped from Jake's grip. The Prada-bedecked young man scooped up a martini shaker from a bar set in the wall, filled it with ice and an array of lip-puckering liqueurs, gave them a rattle, and poured himself what Jake, after his short stint as a bartender, knew to be a green-apple sour. "Let me guess, you're more of a beer man," Alejandro said between sips.

The tone made Jake's hackles rise. Despite his ex-boyfriend's campy persona, or perhaps because of it, Jake was no fan of needlessly cutting zingers. He was desensitized to locker room taunts of "in your face," "that's what she said," and an endless stream of sexual innuendos involving the MILFs of his teammates in impossible positions; it was gay games that drove him crazy. That didn't mean he couldn't play.

Alejandro held the martini glass towards him.

"I'll pass," Jake said, not waiting for an invite to walk down the hall. He wasn't one to fence with words. He established dominance through action, forcing the other two to follow him. For a moment, he started to feel like alpha high-school Jake.

The front hall had worn, peeling wallpaper with faded pink roses. The banister was partially stripped of layers of paint. The kitchen was equally rough.

Checkerboard linoleum curled at the corners; a bare bulb hung above a table; mismatched handles adorned bright pink melamine cabinets. The countertop matched the Barbie hue—except for the handprint burned into its surface. Jake splayed his fingers and pressed his palm into the blackened shape. *Is this a joke?* he wondered.

"Our last pledge didn't work out so well," Alejandro explained. "Bit of a pyro. Now that we don't have to worry about him torching the place, we can renovate this dump."

Alejandro picked up a copy of *Wallpaper*, holding it open to show Jake a sleek kitchen of built-in appliances, granite countertops, and designer cabinets.

"Shiny," Jake said indifferently, opening the rusting fridge. He pushed aside a wall of Veuve and took out a bottle of Etienne water. "Cheers," he said, holding up the water. It was another power play, not asking for the aqua.

I ruled the Nuffim High locker room; I can handle one pissy princess, Jake assured himself.

Alejandro's green eyes bulged. He lunged and yanked the bottle out of Jake's hand. The guy was so fast, the former football star didn't feel the receptacle leave his fingers. So much for the alpha routine.

"Slow down, Arab Axel Rose," Alejandro said. "That's for initiation—*if* you get that far. First, you have to pass the test."

"I can have an appletini, but a bottle of water is a big deal?" Jake scoffed. "Whatever, man."

More games. As much as Jake "straight-acting" Kanaan would have denied it, that meant things were getting interesting. Jake leaned against the battered countertop, spreading his hands as he gripped it; this strategically stretched his shirt against his nipples and made his muscles pop. Alejandro stared. Jake smirked.

MAYBE IT'S TIME TO STOP TRYING TO PROVE YOURSELF WHILE TRYING TO LOOK LIKE YOU'RE IN CONTROL.

Jake's cocky smile cracked. The voice was Felix's, but the handsome youth's lips hadn't moved.

"Our group's elite," Alejandro insisted, putting the water bottle back in the fridge. "Joining changes a man. We need to know what baggage you're carrying. We can't risk you turning into an A-bomb."

Jake recalled his ex's emotional outbursts and replied, "Fair enough."

"Come on," Felix said. "You have to meet Blake."

The name Blake brought to mind visions of an Olympic God of the Slopes, whooshing on his snowboard amidst mountainous moguls, his perfect smile flashing whiter than the spray of the snow in his wake.

When Jake entered the dining room, he met a different kind of Blake. Lying on the floor was an obese young man, barely more than a kid, in pressed sweatpants and T-shirt.

"Sorry," Alejandro said.

"For what?" Jake asked.

Alejandro gestured at Blake. "For Super Size Me."

"Are you being fat-phobic?" Jake chastised. Alejandro shrugged indifferently.

Blake looked up. He held a live blowtorch and wore a pair of protective goggles. A part of the wall was swung back on massive hydraulic hinges. Beyond, Jake spied a small chamber with a slew of computers and monitors. On the dining room wall was a big red button inside a protective case that said, *Push In Case of Emergency.*

"For the love of... this is supposed to be top secret, omega clearance only," Blake cried. The youth turned off the torch and shoved the wall shut. It clicked into place seamlessly. If Jake hadn't seen it, he'd be none the wiser anything was back there.

"It's a panic room," Alejandro said, showing Jake a book with curled corners and highlighted pages.

How to Survive a Robot Uprising; Tips On Defending Yourself Against the Coming Rebellion, Jake read.

"Dork here's afraid of a robot attack," Alejandro explained.

"Hey!" Blake protested, reaching for the book. His fingers slid off the cover like it was Teflon.

"You guys are seriously weird," Jake said.

Felix smiled. "You have no idea. And I think we're okay with this one," Felix said of Jake. "From what I can see, he'll grow in interesting ways."

Jake's spine tightened. Playtime was over. Soon they'd ask for a commitment. He'd have to start giving up who he was to be one of them.

YOU ARE SO FULL OF IT, he heard Felix's voice in his head, but Felix's lips remained perfectly still. *YOU'RE NOT AFRAID OF US TURNING YOU INTO SOMETHING YOU'RE NOT. YOU'RE AFRAID THAT AROUND US, YOU'LL GIVE IN TO WHO YOU ARE.*

Is he a ventriloquist? Jake wondered.

"I should go," he said abruptly. "Blake, don't worry, I know how to keep a secret. And, try to keep these guys from being total douches."

"It's a losing battle," Blake sighed. "Wait, why are you leaving? You seem nice."

"The road calls," Jake replied, giving Blake a friendly salute. "Good luck with the Armageddon."

Blake started after Jake, but Felix held him back.

"This has to be his choice," Felix said

"We didn't get to choose," Blake replied.

"Exactly," Felix concluded.

Jake heard, didn't understand, and didn't care. He bounded out the front door and down the porch steps, hopping into his open-air jeep. *Alejandro's probably making himself a sour-tini and thinking good riddance,* Jake thought.

"Whatever," he muttered to himself, revving the engine.

Condragulations, Kanaan, he chastised his ambivalent attachment pattern, *you've managed to avoid putting down roots in one more place.*

He wheeled the jeep around and got ready to gun the stick shift—if only the way ahead were clear. A black Hummer barreled down the gravel road towards him.

"What the hell?" he said.

The Hummer decked-out Mad Max style—steel plated with thick, metal spikes jutting out from the fender—and headed right for Jake. He tried to accelerate out of the way, but in a nightmarish freeze frame, the spikes smashed into the side of his jeep. Metal ripped through metal with a hair-raising shriek, sending Jake flying. He didn't know what was up or down, what was sky or ground. His Kerouac book flew alongside him. He landed hard, knocking the breath from him, leaving him in pulmonary limbo before air slammed into his lungs.

His chest heaved, and the world snapped into place—only to unleash more chaos.

Chapter 2

A muscular Black woman with a shaved head stepped out of the Hummer. She was G.I. Jane meets Grace Jones.

G.I. Jones was dressed in military pants tucked into polished boots, her strong arms bared in a green tank top. The sun glinted off her aviator glasses. Her leather-gloved hand casually pointed an Uzi at Jake.

He panted under her murderous stare. He was about to die. His greatest regret flashed before his eyes. Her arm moved robotically to the right, Uzi aimed at the three vehicles parked by the edge of the forest. Her finger flexed, unleashing a spray of bullets into the Porsche, truck, and motorcycle.

A cacophony of metal piercing metal sent birds into the air. Windows shattered, tires popped, and gasoline dripped; she fired a single shot, and the tank exploded in a geyser of flame that sent burning rubber into the surrounding woods.

Jake's temples pounded.

What the hell, what the hell, what the—

Strong hands lifted him to his feet.

COME ON MAN, MOVE!

It was Felix's voice, in his head. Jake blinked in a daze.

I SAID MOVE!

The command pierced Jake. His jelly legs grew firm as they ran towards the house. More Uzi fire rose behind them; Jake cringed and covered his ears, heart hammering in terror.

They reached the porch, the clatter of their feet surreal as they bounded up the stairs. Jake turned and watched G.I. Jones striding towards them. She tossed the Uzi aside. It landed with a thud.

She pulled out a Taser.

"Felix," Jake said, trying to back away; Felix held him firm.

"Trust me, as soon as she gets close enough…"

Felix pressed his fingers to his temples.

The woman cringed and missed a step, grasping the side of her head. Gritting her teeth, she forced herself forward.

"You do not want to be swimming around in my head, boy," she said to Felix. "I don't run from my memories."

Her finger squeezed; the Taser nodes flew through the air, embedding themselves in Felix's stomach.

"Oh crap," Felix said, shoving Jake away.

Felix's eyes bulged, and his lips quivered with electricity. As he fell to the veranda, the front door slammed open. Blake yanked the Taser nodes out of Felix and hopped over him, acting as a human shield.

"Get him inside," Blake ordered Jake.

The woman reached the front steps. She fired another round of Taser coils. They embedded themselves into Blake and released volt upon volt. To Jake's surprise, Blake didn't grimace in pain. His expression was one of bliss as the energy rippled through him.

"Yum," he sighed.

Jake watched in awe as Blake's body grew bigger, expanding over the elastic waistband of his sweatpants. His shirt ripped to shreds, and for a moment Jake expected Blake to say, "You make Hulk mad. Hulk smash!" except the young man looked less like an irradiated mountain of muscle and more like Blob of Marvel mutant fame.

The Taser fizzled with a defeated whine. Blake smiled at the attacker. "Payback," he said, slamming his palm against the porch.

Shockwaves rippled outwards. The boards beneath the woman snapped and threw her backwards. She flipped in the air with a gymnast's grace, pulled something from the bag at her side, landed nimbly on her booted feet, and casually slid a gas mask over her face.

A canister spewing a white cloud landed at Blake's feet. "Oh mother," Blake swore as the gas filled his lungs. He teetered, his massive body toppling towards Jake.

He knew this was going to hurt—a lot.

He cursed every stupid decision he'd made that had led him to this moment. He squeezed his eyes shut and shielded Felix from the behemoth toppling towards them—an admirably futile gesture.

Jake heard the slam of Blake hitting the deck. Any moment now the pain would envelop Jake—except it didn't. He opened his eyes. He cradled Felix, the pair of them seemingly unharmed—other than they were sticking up out of Blake's unconscious body. They weren't sitting or standing on him. Their bodies were somehow *inside* Blake, their heads and shoulders sprouting out of him.

And like magic, there was Alejandro, his hand on Jake's shoulder. "Come on," Alejandro said, dragging Jake to his feet. "I can't keep us phased forever, and we do not want to turn solid inside of something else. And for eff's sake, keep hold of Felix!"

Jake obeyed—what else could he do?—helping Alejandro drag Felix's groaning form free of Blake and into the house. *We were inside of him!* Jake's mind raged at the impossibility.

Felix came to, coughing and squirming.

"You okay, babe?" Alejandro asked. Felix managed a moan in response.

Through the open door, Jake saw G.I. Jones crouch, using Blake's fallen bulk for cover, and aim her gun. Alejandro grabbed Jake and pushed him hard.

"Hey!" Jake cried, but instead of banging into the wall he went right through it, Felix and Alejandro along with him. They were in the dining room. They'd passed through a solid wall! Alejandro slammed his palm against the big red *Push In Case of Emergency* button. A steel slab slammed down, blocking the doorway into the dining room. Similar coverings fell into place over the windows, plunging them into darkness until red lights beamed to life from hidden recesses along the moulding.

"I never thought I'd say this, but thank you God for making Blake so damned paranoid," Alejandro said. The floorboards above them creaked. Alejandro stared at the sound. "There's more of them upstairs.

Jake grabbed him by the shoulders.

"What the hell have you gotten me into?" Jake demanded.

Something smashed against the steel barrier, sending a metallic echo running through Jake's spine.

"Sorry chico," Alejandro said, clasping Jake's biceps, "no time to explain."

Alejandro shoved Jake, and they both went right through another wall as if it weren't there, stumbling into Blake's hidden panic room.

"Stay here," Alejandro said, his body still half within the wall. "The door will open automatically once the air starts running out. You should be safe by then. Don't tell anyone about us. No one will believe you."

"Wait. Where are you going?" Jake asked.

"Away from these crazy chicas," Alejandro said, "whoever they are."

He let go of Jake, pulled back, and disappeared from view. Jake dove after him—and slammed against unyielding matter.

"Let me out of here!" he shouted. No one answered. He gazed at a bank of security monitors. They showed a multiplicity of happenings in and around the house.

On one, a crane with a grapple lifted Blake's impossibly massive form into the back of a pickup. *He turned the Taser energy into fat,* Jake thought to himself. On another TV, Alejandro knelt next to Felix. *Alejandro can pass through solid objects; and Felix, his voice was in my head!*

On a third monitor, G.I. Jones attached magnetic clamps to the steel door sectioning off the dining room. Chains linked the clamps to the Mad Max Hummer outside. Jake pulled out his phone, ready to dial 9-1-1.

YOU DON'T WANT TO DO THAT.

It was Felix's voice. Jake didn't bother looking for speakers. The panic room was a sound-proofed bubble of silence.

THE POLICE CAN'T HELP US.

Jake pressed 9 on his phone.

YOU HAVE TO LISTEN TO ME! Felix's voice boomed so loud Jake stumbled back.

On a monitor, he saw the customized Hummer shoot fire from a propulsion unit, and the beast of a machine lurched forward, yanking on the chains. It shook the entire fraternity, ripped out the steel door protecting the dining room, along with most of the wall. On a pair of monitors, Jake saw Alejandro knocked off his feet; he fell through the floor and into the basement.

THAT HAPPENS WHEN HE GETS SURPRISED. HE JUST SLIPS AWAY.

Again, Felix's voice. Jake uselessly covered his ears.

I'M TOO WEAK TO STOP THEM. THERE'S TOO MANY. BUT YOU, YOU HAVE TO WARN THE OTHERS.

"Others?" Jake asked.

A rush of images filled his mind.

There was a muscled wrestler in a singlet, approaching a matted floor in what looked like a high-school gym. The preppy part in his hair was picture perfect—as if shaped in a mold. The image morphed into a spindly freshman pushing his thick glasses up his nose as he rolled an octagonal die. He blurred; a pair of cheerleaders pumping their pompoms came into focus. One was a girl, Asian, pretty and petite; the other was an effete muscular Latinx young man with hair bleached blond. Jake's heart beat faster.

THEY'LL BE NEXT, Felix warned.

Jake swayed, and the cheerleaders dissolved. He shook his head and wiped the sweat from his brow. His Guns N' Roses shirt was drenched. He breathed heavily, the air warm and acrid. His deodorant had given up.

On a monitor, he watched G.I. Jones tying, gagging, and throwing a tarp over Blake's frame. In the basement, a woman with a buzz-cut, a slew of earrings, Eloquii jeans, and a T-shirt that read "Not Here to Be Palatable" shot a dart into Alejandro's back. It must have been a tranquilizer because Alejandro fell to the ground. The woman tossed him over her shoulder and casually carried his limp form up the stairs.

In the kitchen, a third woman with the arms of a butcher and the face of a boxer yanked open the fridge and shoved aside bottles of Veuve. They shattered against the floor. She pulled free the case of Etienne water Jake had tried to drink from less than an hour ago.

She brought it into the dining room, stepped over Felix's prostrate body, and set the case on the table. G.I. Jones and the attacker from the basement joined her; the latter dumped Alejandro next to his boyfriend. Last to enter was a sprite of a woman with delicately spun features wearing a peaked general's visor cap atop a mass of curly hair, a form-fitting lace-embroidered military jacket, tasseled earrings dangling from her ears, and a choker with a glinting black stone about her neck. The effect was *War and Peace* meets *Fifty Shades of Grey*.

She knelt next to Felix and gently touched his head. It was almost motherly. *This can't be real*, Jake thought. *It can't.*

To prove it to himself, he lifted his fist to pound on the wall.

DON'T!

Felix's voice hit the insides of Jake's mind with such intensity Jake stumbled against a control panel. There was a click and hiss of air as the hidden door opened a fraction. The bubble of silence broke.

"Did you hear that?" one of the women asked from the dining room.

Jake's heart pounded harder.

Is this all part of an elaborate hazing? he wondered.

"There was a newb," he heard another woman say.

"You're sure?"

"Has to have been juiced," chimed a third voice, tinged with testosterone. "No way he got away otherwise."

"Great. One more of the little faggots to hunt down."

"Raven!" a sweet sounding one chastised G.I. Jones. "That's the oppressor's language!"

"Right," Raven replied. "Sorry babe."

"Question is," the sugary-voiced one continued, "*did* he get away? Desirée?"

"Checking," baritone Desirée replied.

Jake heard a beeping that grew louder and faster as the creaking floorboards announced someone approaching. Jake watched on a monitor as the woman with the spray of earrings stood right in front of the hidden chamber. She held up her phone, moving it in the air, searching.

Where'd she get an App that does that? Jake wondered.

The wall was open by a sliver—was that enough to give him away? The seconds ticked by.

To hell with this. Jake was ready to slam the door outwards, quads clenched to make a run for it.

STAY, Felix's voice ordered, telling him to do the thing he was worst at.

"Room's clean," the woman grunted.

DON'T MAKE A SOUND, Felix said. *I CLOUDED HER MIND ONCE. I DON'T HAVE IT IN ME TO DO IT AGAIN. DO NOT GET CAUGHT. YOU'RE OUR OBI-WAN.*

I'm your only hope? Jake asked in his mind, not liking the sound of that.

There was no answer. *Felix?* Jake mentally called out.

Idiot, he rolled his eyes. Felix was *not* a telepath. It had all been Jake's panic-stricken imagination. Yet, when Felix didn't reply, it wasn't just silent in Jake's mind; it was as if someone had left the room.

On a monitor, he noticed Desirée injecting something into Felix's forearm.

"That'll keep him out of our heads," she said.

"Right on schedule," the pretty one replied, busily typing away on her phone.

"Recalibrating mission parameters?" Raven asked.

"Updating social media status," the petite one replied, poking away at the touchscreen. "Mission Accomplished. You all better click Like."

"One last detail," the one with the boxer's nose said, jerking her head towards the bottles of water on the dining room table.

"Let's make sure there are no more Newbies to hunt down," Raven said.

"We're not hunting," the Pixie chided. "That's so patriarchal."

"Athena was a hunter," Raven said. She wilted under the petite woman's stern gaze.

"We have a higher purpose," the little redhead said.

Jake heard a multitude of ch-ch sounds as the women cocked their guns, and he watched on a monitor as Raven pointed her weapon at the bottled water. The other women came to stand next to her, each of them drawing their firearms.

"Womyn of Wonder, do we have consensus?" the little one asked.

"We do," the other three responded in unison. They opened fire.

Plastic bottles flew everywhere amidst showers of aqua; clear liquid ran down the leg of the dining room table and pooled on its surface. Jake covered his ears. Bang! Bang! Bang! It went on until one last plastic water bottle flew into the air. Raven fired a single shot, blowing it apart and spraying water all over the carpet of spent shells covering the wooden floor.

They blasted bottled water? Jake wondered. How did that make any sense?

The scariest one, Raven, bound Felix's wrists and ankles. All the while, she kept staring at Jake's hiding spot.

"Raven?" the petite one in the military cap asked. "What is it?"

Raven held up her phone. There was a long pause.

Oh, shit, Jake thought, clenching his fists. Any thought of revealing himself disappeared amidst the carnage they'd unleashed. He looked at the controls of Blake's hidden room, wondering which one would close the door.

Raven shook her phone. "It's out of juice. They need to make better batteries for these things."

"We'll make our own," the red head replied, standing on tiptoe as they kissed.

Jake released his bunched biceps. His chest dripped sweat. Raven dragged Felix out by the collar. The woman with the spray of earrings did the same to Alejandro. The others followed. Jake heard their military boots clapping on the hardwood. Their laughter grew faint.

Jake watched on a monitor as they drove off with Felix and Alejandro in the Hummer and Blake in the pickup. The truck's muffler belched in protest.

Jake's physique was a frozen tableau, haunted by the throbbing in his head and the patter of perspiration plopping to the floor.

They're gone, he assured himself. *You can move now.*

He pushed the door open on its semi-circular hinges. His head turned on a swivel, taking in the torn-up dining room. One wall was a shattered mess where the steel door had been ripped from its hinges. The metal slab lay at an awkward angle, blocking the kitchen. Part of the ceiling had fallen in, baring the rafters, and bits of insulation drifted in the air. The dining room table was little more than shards. Bullet holes filled one wall. Slaughtered Etienne water bottles lay where they'd fallen.

But why?

Jake crouched and dabbed at the water pooled around one of the table legs.

"Because of this," he said. There was something out of the ordinary about it, dangerous even.

What was it Alejandro had said when Jake had tried to help himself to a bottle of water from the fridge? *That's for initiates only.* Could something so banal be responsible for the incredible things Felix and his friends could do?

"That could've been me," Jake said. Relief arm-wrestled disappointment. The power those boys possessed set them apart; it also bound them together.

I have to get out of here, he knew.

His rubber soles plonked in the water and kicked aside bullet shells as he headed for the door. He was almost out of the gay fraternity—but not quite. A Kerouac quote whispered to him, *Walking on water wasn't built in a day.*

"Unless it was," Jake whispered back. He stared at the steel door yanked from its hinges. More specifically, he stared at what lay tucked in its shadow.

He dropped to his knees in front of the slab, and his fingers closed around a bottle of Etienne water. He held it up. It was whole and untouched.

He wandered in a daze, out onto the porch. He saw the burnt handprint on the doorframe with new understanding. There were more of *them* out there.

He thought about calling the police as he descended the steps; or he could go back to university and join a real fraternity; maybe he should escape on another around the world trip—whatever it took to forget this nightmare.

He held the aqua up to the setting sun. *This is crazy. It's just a bottle of water,* he assured himself. *This isn't some comic book with a mad scientist potion that turned these homos into into heroes.*

And yet, what the gayternity brothers could do…

Jake cracked open the lid.

Pour it out, he ordered himself. He tilted the bottle towards the muddy ground and stared at his Kerouac book. It had been thrown from the car and now lay singed at his feet. Kerouac spoke.

The only people for me are the mad ones, the ones who are mad to live, mad to talk, mad to be saved, desirous of everything at the same time, the ones who never yawn or say a commonplace thing, but burn, burn, burn…

With that, Jake Kanaan drank the water down.

Chapter 3

Troy Allstar was a paradox.

The teen was a jacked Ken doll come to life—the perfect fit for his senior seller position at the Nuffim Mall's Aberbombie and Stitch clothing store.

"Understood sir," he said into his headset, "need to clear out waffled long sleeves for next week's shipment of distressed denim. On it!"

He received and acted on his manager's instructions with the same focused intensity as he would his coach's plays before heading onto the football field or taking down an opponent at a wrestling match.

"Van, Touchdown, Shellshocked," he called out, corralling his floor staff with two snaps of his fingers. Their real names were Jim, Jamal, and Junaid, but according to Diesel, the store manager, those names weren't "Aberbombie enough," and he'd rebranded them. Now, they sounded like video game characters.

"Come on," Troy insisted, "let's put some muscle into the hustle. Quit sexting and start selling."

The generically hot trio looked suitably sheepish while making their cell phones disappear into their overly tight jeans.

"Can we talk to customers about the new Halo?" Shellshocked/Jamal asked. "The jetpack enhancements are awesome."

Troy had to admit, Diesel had given the guy an apt codename.

"Only if you can work in our two-for-one sale."

Even without cleats, padded shoulders, or a singlet, Troy exuded team captain. Dressed in a ribbed tank with the words "Spring Fever" beneath his large pecs, and a pair of plaid shorts that rounded over his backside, it was as if he'd stepped out of one the posters adorning the store's walls.

And that's where the paradox came in. The store's ads all carried the requisite Aberbombie homoerotic undertones. The key word was "undertones." The brand's odes to boy-boy love were restricted to shades of grey, even when cast in black-and-white prints of two jocks wrestling in the mud in their torn underwear.

The lesson? Male touching was profitable, but only if it came within the confines of boyish play. All that described Troy to a T—until he turned into a Q.

He walked to the shirtless greeter at the front of the store and kissed him on the mouth. Enter Troy's boyfriend, Chad García. Chad was the personification of the archetype Jung had failed to recognize—a smooth-bodied Latinx muscle twink with bleached surfer hair and a flair for the dramatic.

The mall was packed, offering a capacity audience for today's *Troy and Chad Show*. A grandmother hobbling by on a walker flashed them a toothless grin; a trio of cheerleaders forgot about the pink belly shirts on sale, gazing teary-eyed and clasping their hands as if to say, "Edward and Bella who?" Even school-jerk Markham, whose fists targeted anyone who stepped outside the narrow confines of his Wonder Bread world order, put a hand on his towering goon Riley and sighed romantically, "Let's go beat up some geeks."

Troy pulled away, smiling at Chad. "Hey BF," Troy said.

"Hey, yourself," the shorter youth replied.

The unexpected kiss put a goofy grin on Chad's face as his boyfriend turned back into the store and got caught in a whirlwind of retail detail. The tanks and crewnecks were on the same display table, messing up the pricing. An eyeball was missing from the giant moose head over the cashiers' counter. And, horror of horrors, last year's giant foam core poster had been mistakenly placed in the front entrance, depicting a bikini-clad nymphette, awkwardly inserted between two buff boys on a tartan blanket in the middle of a swaying barley field.

It was Chad who'd noticed that faux pas.

"So two seasons ago," he'd said.

He watched his man in action, barking orders into his headset. Under Troy's leadership, all the wrinkles were ironed out—crewnecks moved, ping pong ball coated in black marker popped into the animal trophy's skull, and the new season's ad of frolicking beach bros in boxer briefs slid into place—just in time. The store's manager, Diesel, returned, sucking on a straw stabbed into a plastic cup with a thick green concoction in it.

"Matcha tea booster," he explained, once again turning himself into the living embodiment of a nobody-asked meme.

Diesel's wavy brown hair was swept back in a style reminiscent of James Dean. With his tan skin and crisp collar underneath a hoodie, Diesel looked ready to move into a cabin in the woods—one that was complete with hair-dryer, Wi-Fi, and a juicer.

16

"All right boys and girls," Diesel said to his staff, "listen up."

No one was surprised when he began to wax poetic about PROWL, Aberbombie's new scent. What did surprise Chad was that Troy wasn't paying attention. He gazed out at the mall, a worried furrow to his brow.

"You can get Botox for that," Chad joked.

"What?" Troy asked from a million mental miles away.

"Never mind," Chad blushed. Troy still had a way of making him feel nervous. He wanted to ask Troy what was bothering him, but Troy didn't like questions like that. He'd been so affectionate earlier; Chad didn't want to risk making him withdraw.

"There's PROWL for HIM and PROWL for HER," Diesel intoned, holding a pair of bottles in the shapes of Tarzan and Jane. "Aberbombie is equal opportunity, especially when it comes to prowling."

Chad stifled a yawn. His job was to say hello and goodbye. Spritzing the new scent would fall to someone else. But, as greeter, he did feel certain obligations. Chad stuck out his hand and grabbed hold of what seemed to be nothing.

"Mandy," he said with a prim and chastising voice.

Her invisible form appeared within his grip. She held a spaghetti-strap Aberbombie tank with the words *Sparkle* in glittery letters.

"Again?" Chad asked.

She shrugged. "Can I help it if turning invisible makes me the world's best shoplifter?"

"How'd you get the security tag off?" he asked.

"Forcefield," she shrugged. "If I apply it just right, those security do-hickies drop off like our friendship after you got into a new relationship."

"Really?" he asked, ignoring the jab and considering the free clothes possibilities of his best friend's ability to go unseen.

"There's some great new stuff at Armani Exchange. Way more your style than this generic, body-shaming jock crap. My treat," she winked.

Chad nodded, then shook his head, banishing the temptation. "This is so not you."

"You don't know," Mandy snapped.

"I kind'a do. The only time you try the five-finger discount is here, when I'm working, when you know I can smell you not really trying to sneak by." He took the shirt from her hand and rolled his eyes. "This isn't your size."

Her pretty jaw jutted. "Fine. I've been served. But it's the only way I get to see you now that you've moved to Couplesville, population not-me."

"Mandy, I'm sorry for bailing on you last night—"

"And the night before that," she added, folding her arms over her chest.

"You've dated all through high school—"

"And part of junior too. Started in grade four. Dated a fifth grader. No biggie, even if all the girls were jealous," she added in an offhand way, still refusing to look at him.

"Exactly. This is my *first* real relationship. For me, this *is* a big deal."

"This is so not your first relationship. There was—"

Chad cut her off. "Douche Bag Who Shall Not Be Named doesn't count."

"I don't see why not," she countered, tapping her foot impatiently.

"Because he was in the closet," Chad explained. "I felt lonelier with him than without him. And you remember how pathetically lonely I was without him. With Troy, I get to have a proper relationship."

That made her shoulders cave. "I hate it when you remind me of that. It's all so romantic and *Paris is Burning* and stuff."

"You do realize that's a documentary about New York trans and drag voguing house culture, *not* a chick flick set in the city of love, right?"

"Save it for IMDB. Just tell me you've figured out who wrote that note in Troy's journal," Mandy said, pulling out the Paris Hilton *Your Heiress Diary* that Chad had given to his man.

"Mandy!" Chad snapped. "Where did you get that?"

"Your boyfriend's night table. Top drawer. Duh! Here's a tip," she opened to a page of advice from Paris Hilton, quoting it. "*Write it down when you have a good-hair day. You'll want to remember it when you're having a bad one.*" Mandy snapped the journal shut. "Heiresses are so wise."

"Give it," Chad said reaching for the book.

Mandy's forcefield snapped on; Chad yanked his hand back. "So I guess you don't want to know what Troy filled in on page 154," Mandy said.

"Uh… No," Chad replied.

"It's the *My Ideal Guy* page," Mandy said, "but whatever."

Chad rubbed his knuckles where they'd banged on his best friend's forcefield.

"Suit yourself," Mandy shrugged. "You're a better person than I am. Besides, he's barely written in this thing since you gave it to him. Why would he? Everything's going his way now that he can control everyone's emotions."

18

"What's that supposed to mean?" Chad asked.

"Nothing," she said in a way that meant something. "Here, smell and tell me who wrote this. It's driving me crazy, like, I need treat day *now* crazy."

Chad stared at the words written in the diary. *They know who you are, and they know what you can do. They came for us, now they're coming for you.*

It had been a month since they'd found the warning in the journal Chad had bought for Troy, a month of waiting for something to happen, for someone to come for them because they'd developed superpowers. It had turned into a month of nothing.

"I told you already—" Chad began.

"I know, no scent. Just try it one more time. Please?" Mandy begged.

Chad could see the stress on his friend's face.

"Fine," he said. "But only 'cause I loves you."

He inhaled deeply where the mysterious message was written. A flood of scents filtered and separated within him—the glue from the binding, the acid in the paper, the ink from the pen, a volley of people who'd touched it on the discount table before Chad bought it. There was also the scent of Mandy, Troy, and Troy's little brother Gibbie, all of whom had handled it—and something else; something he'd missed before, camouflaged by the overpowering cologne Chad sprayed on it before giving it to Troy.

The cologne was a mere breeze now, evaporated as time had passed, and underneath…

"What? What do you smell?" Mandy asked.

"Someone familiar," Chad said, but it was too faint to nail down.

"Useless," Mandy said, grabbing the diary.

"Mandy, is this an Aspartame crash?" Chad chided.

"I think I'm justified in not wanting to sit around waiting for someone to come for us," Mandy said.

"Look," Chad reassured her, "Troy says everything's fine."

"Chad, just because Troy says things are fine, does not mean that things are fine."

Chad's head jerked as if slapped. When Troy said things were fine, that's *exactly* how they were, and Chad's anxiety melted away. That made Chad pause. Troy was what Gibbie called a "projecting empath," which meant he could sense and control other people's emotions. Surely, Troy wasn't using his powers on his boyfriend. He wouldn't do that—would he?

The thought filled Chad with worry, and immediately Troy's head swung towards him.

"…and it's critical we get across to the Aberbombieites the essence of our new scent," Diesel explained. "It's like the soft tread of a cougar moving through a wooded glen…"

"You okay?" Troy came over and asked Chad.

"I'm…" Chad was about to explain his worries that, without realizing it, Troy might be using his power to alter emotions on the one person who loved him more than anything. The words were on Chad's lips, but Troy touched him on the small of the back, and the cheerleader's unease dissipated as it always did when his boyfriend was around. "I'm fine," Chad said with a contented sigh.

"Interesting," Mandy snipped, but Chad didn't hear.

Troy smiled at him, the smile that made Chad melt—and that made him worry. Were things *too* perfect?

Today is a good hair day, Chad comforted himself.

He just wasn't sure about tomorrow.

Chapter 4

Across from Aberbombie and Stitch was the store Games and Geeks.

While Aberbombie was the muster station for jocks and Valley girls, Games and Geeks was a haven for misfits like Carl and Matt, who'd found an escape from ridicule in flights of the fantastic. Within these walls, spaceships jumped to distant points using faster-than-light drives; a queen determined to win back her throne lost her dragons, and an aberrant twist in DNA transformed measly teenagers into super-powered heroes—and villains.

"Where the hell is Gibbie?" Matt asked, tossing a set of clattering dice onto the table before him.

Matt's pale white form stretched a bland sweat top that favored comfort over style.

"Not with us," Carl replied, braces sparkling and mouth swishing with foamed almond milk from a 20-pump vanilla latte. The young Asian bore a baseball cap with a space academy insignia on the forehead. He was a freshman, like Matt and Gibbie, with twig arms, a keyboarder's slouch, and a determination to use his IQ to become bigger than Bill Gates.

The Games and Geeks clientele varied from that of Aberbombie and Stitch, but the two stores had more in common than first blush might suggest.

The full-sized cut out of Princess Leia in her iconic Jabba the Hut slave outfit was similar in intent to Aberbombie's nymphets in Daisy Duke shirts and cut-off shorts—each commodifying the female form through fantasy and fetish. And while Carl and Matt were classic examples of Games and Geeks' patrons, their sallow likeness lacked representation on the walls surrounding them. Arnold Schwarzenegger flexed pre-gubernatorial pecs while brandishing barbarian justice in a Conan poster. He-Man's muscled physique crackled with lighting as he called forth the power of Greyskull. Even nerdy Peter Parker had abs. Swap in some branded underwear and these jacked heroes became an Aberbombie wet dream.

"Have you noticed Gibbie's been late a lot these days? And he'll cancel at the last minute," Matt pressed, jumping his wizard over the Lava Fields of Icarus on the game board before him. "Magi casts Spell of Frozen Lake."

"Gibbie's caught in the gravity well of his increasingly dense ego," Carl agreed. "Demons of the Deep counter Frozen Lake Spell with Shield of Primus."

"Even when he's here, he's *not* here, you know?" Matt added, handing Carl the dice. They clattered from the boy's bony hand.

"His presence has become redundant at best," Carl agreed.

"I even miss him pining after Chad," Matt sighed, handing a plastic gem to Carl. He rubbed it between his hands and muttered "precious," under his breath.

They approached their games with the strategic vigor of elite athletes. Unfortunately, not every battle came down to a roll of the dice. Case in point, pretty boy Markham (who'd given Matt a slew of self-worth eroding nicknames) led his goon Riley into the comic book—and not to browse the merch.

In days past, the two football players would've brazenly marched in. Now, they looked about skittishly as if for potential danger. Satisfied that their favorite holding pen contained potential victims, free of anyone with the brawn to stop them, the pair puffed up and nodded to each other cockily.

They sauntered past the register, ignored by the store clerk. She was a spectacled librarian type, petite with long curly red hair and pale white skin sprinkled with freckles. She wore a green T-shirt with the words *Witness the power of this fully armed and operational battle station.* She busily typed on her phone, her free hand playing with a metallic black stone hanging from her neck while Tegan and Sara blasted from her headphones. She was oblivious to Markham and Riley as they loomed over her patrons.

"Hey nerds," Markham said, followed by Riley's ogre laugh.

Matt fell backward and scrambled away. Carl hopped to his feet, using his chair as a shield.

"Man, I've missed this," Markham said. He breathed deep—as if fear were his oxygen. Riley grabbed the table with the board game and was about to flip the whole thing over.

"Don't worry," Carl whispered to Matt, "I've got it memorized."

"Like the time you tried to give yourself an extra thousand gold coins because you thought I wasn't keeping track?" Matt whispered back.

Riley grinned, lifting the table and thinking how beautiful the sound of destruction was going to be.

"I wouldn't do that if I were you," a voice cracked behind them.

Markham and Riley turned to face a gawky redhead with thick glasses, stained jeans, and a black sweat top with a red V. He slurped his Big Gulp through a straw.

The massive Riley swallowed hard and lowered the table. A nervous grin crested his pug face.

"Oh, hey Gibbie," Riley said. "Didn't see you there. I was, uh…"

Gibbie threw his empty cup towards a trash bin. The cup missed and hit the floor. Everyone stared at it, including the sprite-like woman behind the cash. Gibbie folded his arms over his pigeon chest.

"Pick it up," Gibbie said.

Markham and Riley looked at each other.

"Now!" Gibbie shouted.

Markham pushed Riley, and the big oaf slunk over and put the fallen cup into the trash. It hardly seemed possible, yet the emaciated youth had cowed these primitive buffoons. The woman with fiery red hair took off her headphones and watched with growing interest. Markham noticed her noticing, making him blush.

"Whatever," he said, trying to step past Gibbie.

Gibbie grasped him by the arm, and no matter how much Markham tried to pull away, the smaller teen held him fast.

"I think you should stay," Gibbie said.

"How the hell are you so damn strong?" Markham cursed, unable to break free.

"You said you were here to play," Gibbie taunted.

"I never said that," Markham replied.

"You're right. I did. That means you're here to play. You," Gibbie said to Riley, making the giant flinch, "you can go."

Riley didn't need to be told twice. As loyal as he was, and despite Markham's glare, Riley shuffled off.

"There a problem?" Gibbie asked.

"Hell no," Markham said with false cheer, "let's do this thing."

"Let's," Gibbie agreed, forcing Markham into a chair at the table with Carl and Matt, who were looking to each other uncomfortably.

Markham yanked his arm free—he suspected Gibbie let him—and adjusted his jacket around his broad shoulders.

"I guess I'll be this guy," he said, reaching for a game piece of a muscular barbarian dressed in a loincloth and brandishing a laser pistol.

23

Carl's eyes bulged, and he grabbed Markham's wrist.

"That's General Chewlock. It's taken me three years to build up his experience points," Carl sputtered.

Markham looked ready to smack the kid. Gibbie coughed loudly. Grimacing irritably, Markham put the statuette back on the board.

"You can be Deriscia." Gibbie offered him a pinky-sized figurine of a voluptuous green woman with quadruple breasts and devil horns. "She's a Weslinian love slave. She's got tons of experience points."

Matt snorted, and Carl wheezed with mirth.

"Awesome," Markham slouched.

The redhead behind the counter watched the whole thing. Markham looked at the floor. "Just get through this, O'Reilly," he muttered to himself and rolled the dice. They rattled on the table as Gibbie sat down at the counter to read a comic book.

"You were a little rough on him, don't you think?" the cashier asked.

"Who? Markham?" Gibbie asked.

"What do you mean I can't lure Captain Chewlock off the bridge?" Markham demanded of Matt and Carl.

"You rolled a two," Matt replied, "and you have a seduction rating of eight. You'd be lucky to make out with a fangor beast."

"He's made my life hell for years," Gibbie said. He read her name tag. *Pixie.*

"Let me guess," Pixie said. "Noogies, head in the toilet, and stuffed into your locker more than once. Now, it's payback time?"

"Kind of," Gibbie admitted.

The conversation made Gibbie nervous. He sometimes forgot to keep his super strength a secret. Using it on Markham was one thing, but showing off, well, Troy had warned him about that. Gibbie told this woman what he'd told Matt and Carl.

"I got tired of it, so I got a black belt in karate," Gibbie lied.

At that point, Mandy traipsed in and walked up to him. Her timing usually sucked; for once, she was right where he needed her—to the rescue.

"We need to talk," she said, ignoring the red-headed cashier. Tucked under Mandy's arm was Troy's Paris Hilton journal.

Gibbie eyed it, knowing about the warning written inside.

"Sure," he said, glad to get away from Pixie's interrogation.

"Hold on," the redhead said, putting her hand on top of Gibbie's, "unless you're going to use your 'karate' on me too."

"What?" Gibbie replied, horrified. "Of course not."

"Good. You go play with the others," Pixie said to Mandy. "That's a dear."

Mandy readied to unleash a verbal blast, but Gibbie shook his head in warning.

"Feeble," Mandy snorted, her heels clicking on the laminate flooring. She lowered herself with the poise of a dancer into the empty seat between Carl and Matt.

"Bathe ever?" she asked, wrinkling her nose at them.

"Yeah, guys," Markham snorted. "There's this thing called deodorant."

He held his hand to Mandy for a high five; she gave him a sour 'we are not friends' face and took out her Channel perfume. She spritzed Carl twice, followed by Matt. They coughed and waved the air in front of their faces.

"I'm allergic to scents!" Carl whined.

"Not your own, clearly," Mandy said, sitting sideways and not looking at any of them.

"You can play with us if you want," Matt offered. His eyes were giant moons as he gazed at Mandy. "You can be Selestra the Vampire Empress."

"Why can't I be Selestra?" Markham demanded.

Mandy put on a show of admiring her fingernails as if they were the most interesting things at this table. In her mind, they were. "You're talking to me. Don't."

"Your turn," Carl said, handing Markham the dice. He tossed them onto the board and rolled double zeros.

"Is it just me or does life suck now that everyone's come out?" Markham asked, slumping in his chair, his letterman jacket bunching up around his neck.

"Tell me about it," Mandy said. He looked at her plaid skirt riding up her thigh.

She noticed and pulled down the hem. He shrugged. "You're damaged goods anyway. I can't believe I asked you to prom." He glanced at Gibbie wilting under Pixie's stern gaze.

"Maybe things are looking up," Markham said. Not one to let an opportunity pass, Markham stood, saluting Matt and Carl with a middle finger.

"Later losers," he said.

As Markham began his exit, he found some of his old cockiness, putting a strut in his step. Gibbie clenched his fist and took a threatening step towards him. Markham chirped and stumbled into a carousel of pulp fiction. He struggled—and failed—to keep a few books from falling to the floor then bolted as fast he could. The red-haired nymph appraised Gibbie gloating.

"Must feel good pushing that guy around," she said.

"It doesn't suck," Gibbie admitted.

"That's what I thought," she said sadly. "Gibbie Allstar, you have to learn that superpowers don't give you special rights."

"What?" Gibbie asked, turning to face her.

"Don't play coy," Pixie said. "We know who you are, and we know what you can do."

The words made Gibbie blanch. "You came for them—" he said.

"And now," Pixie agreed, pointing a tranquilizer gun at him, "we've come for you."

Chapter 5

Matt, Carl, and Mandy had not yet noticed Gibbie's danger.

"Do you want to be the Slave Woman from Arkenhhall?" Matt asked Mandy; she was busy picking non-existent lint off her skirt and muttering about "men."

"Really?" she said to Matt. "Talking to me? Again?" She got up and walked towards Gibbie.

"Okay, old woman," she said to Pixie, "chit-chat time's over. Gibbie's coming with—"

"Uh, Mandy," Gibbie said, his hands in the air.

The red-haired cashier aimed the dart gun at Mandy.

"This is *beyond* feeble," Mandy said.

The dart fired with a twang and bounced off Mandy's flickering blue force shield.

"How did you—" Pixie said in complete surprise.

"And just you wait until Gibbie kicks the crap out of you," Mandy snorted. "Gibbie?"

He was collapsed over the counter. She turned to see a second woman, her ear loaded with gold rings.

"She's one of them!" Pixie shouted in warning, pointing at Mandy.

"But I thought—" the other woman began.

"Desirée, just shoot!" Pixie ordered.

Desirée fired a Taser. Mandy's field flared, and the weapon bounced off. With a growl, Mandy made the shield pulse outwards, smacking the newcomer and Pixie off their feet. It wasn't enough to knock them out, but they were stunned. Matt and Carl were slumped over their board game, tranquilizer darts stuck in their backs.

Pixie and her companion struggled to their feet.

"How can you be one of them?" the redhead asked. "You're female."

"Uh, you can't sum me up by my gender," Mandy replied. "I'm *head* cheerleader." She flipped her hair, helped Gibbie to his feet, and turned them both invisible.

Back at Aberbombie and Stitch, Troy Allstar gazed around the store. The hairs on the back of his neck itched. Something was wrong. He'd been feeling it all day. Someone was out to get him—probably some homophobe. He'd tried drawing the person out by publicly kissing Chad, but that had done nothing.

Troy's eyes fell on a poster of muddy lacrosse players facing off on a rainy field, and he felt a shadow closing in.

"This is Raven St. Clair, from Aberbombie corporate," Diesel said, introducing the woman at his side.

Troy gazed at Raven's shaved head, power suit, and a red skinny tie pulled tight enough to choke her. Troy got the sense that was the only way she felt comfortable.

Respect, he thought.

"Your sales figures are impressive," she said, "especially since you were recently on the verge of being fired."

"I guess that's what I needed to get motivated," Troy said cautiously.

Her emotions were like a coiled spring, winding tighter and tighter. It was as if she were bunching up to…

She shoved a Taser into Troy's abdomen. Blue jolts of electricity dropped him to the ground.

"What the hell?" Diesel demanded. "What kind of performance punishment is this?"

"Shut it, muscle boy," Raven said. She stabbed a needle into the side of Diesel's neck and depressed the syringe. His bulky body wavered and toppled like a drunken gorilla.

Shoppers screamed and ran. Raven spoke into the watch on her wrist.

"Romeo is down, repeat, Romeo is down. Require extraction."

A paramedic with a nose that spoke of time in a boxing ring ran in, pushing a gurney with her buff arms.

"It's all right, folks," she said, "everything's under control!"

She and Raven got Troy up on the gurney. His eyes fluttered, and he grabbed the paramedic.

"You want to let me go," he said.

"I do want to let you go," she said with confusion. She began to undo the strap about his ankle.

"Damn it, Chantal!" Raven cursed, grabbing a syringe and jabbing the needle into Troy's arm.

"You don't want to do that," Troy warned with a growl, sending pain through her body. He felt her suffering, enough to make anyone else pass out, but this woman grit her teeth and forced herself through the agony.

"Nice try, boy," she said. She squeezed the syringe, and Troy's polished Aberbombie empire was sucked into a slum of dank darkness.

Raven panted as Troy's eyes fluttered shut. She'd known what he could do, but experiencing it first hand was something else. She finished strapping him to the gurney. His hyper-gelled hair remained glued in place. She looked forward to shaving him bald.

"Big mistake, lady."

Raven turned and faced the most beautiful youth she'd ever seen. She immediately had a *Fight Club* moment.

"I want to break something pretty," she smiled, cracking her knuckles and launching into action.

She was fast; this kid was faster. Before she could complete a step, he closed the distance between them and smashed his fist across her jaw. The blow sent her flying over the gurney, ramming her into a display of chunky savannah sweaters. Shelves crunched and toppled onto her. Pretty boy was fast *and* strong.

"This is going to be fun," she said.

Chantal fired a tranquilizer dart at the youth. He caught it in midair and threw it back at her with blinding speed. She ducked, and it pierced a floor-to-ceiling tableau, right in the crotch of a muscular rugby player.

"Get Romeo out of here," Raven shouted at the phony paramedic.

"But—"

"Do it!" Raven got to her feet and charged.

Chad saw the paramedic taking away his unconscious man. His ears grew pointed, and his pupils turned into vertical slits. He growled and loped after his prey on all fours. Raven dove after him, grabbed him by the ankle, and yanked him back. His sharp nails skittered on the polished floor. Fast as an Ultimate Fighting Champion, her fingers snared his hair and smashed his face against a marble countertop.

He was dazed, but only for a moment. His claws slashed her across the belly. She didn't flinch. Chad howled. Her shirt and tie were shredded, but there was no blood. He shook his aching wrist.

"That hurt," he gasped.

29

"Kevlar," she shrugged, patting her vest. She grabbed him by the throat. His nails dug deep into her forearm. She cursed and released him. He somersaulted, landed, and bit her leg.

She aimed her tranquilizer gun and fired. He was gone. The projectile warbled in the floor. He was on the counter, crouched, kicking her in the throat. She unleashed a frenzy of Tae Kwon Do meets Cage Match death strokes that would've been too bloody for the Fight Network—if she could land a punch.

At first, she figured he must have martial arts training, but it was too unformed, too wild.

This is all instinct, she realized in wonder.

She shifted from judo to kickboxing, and he threw her moves back at her. His defense was sloppy, but his speed, strength, and agility made up for it. He didn't need to block because he easily dodged.

Worse, she was getting tired. Not him. Despite the sweat covering his pecs, his abs weren't breathing hard. A panicked thought occurred to her.

I might lose. She *never* lost.

In desperation, she grabbed the display shelf of PROWL and toppled it in front of him. Cologne bottles shattered, and a cloud of perfume engulfed him. He choked and gasped. Her fists and feet pummeled him with unchecked fury. He swung in desperation. She caught his wrist and jabbed a needle into his shoulder. He yowled.

"Don't feel bad kid," she assured him. "I'm bigger, I'm faster, and I will always beat you."

She hated the homo penchant for camp, but damn if she wasn't a Joan Crawford fan. Getting mad at dirt à la *Mommie Dearest* was something Raven could understand. She smiled. "Say goodnight, pretty boy."

"Good night, pretty boy," another male voice responded.

She saw the fist from the corner of her eye and then stars as it smashed into her. She didn't get a good look at him, but he had a mean right hook. Through blurry eyes, she made out a handsome face capped by curly hair buzzed on the sides. The dude's buff bod was dressed in a cut-off shirt with a deep V, tight jeans, and faux diamond earrings that glistened in the store's ambient light.

"Jake?" Chad said with disbelief, shaking his head as if to clear this mirage.

"Hey, kiddo," Jake replied.

Jake crouched beside Chad and pulled the needle from his body, tossing it aside. Raven watched it skitter away. She hadn't had time to depress it.

Crap, she thought. This was going from bad to apocalyptic.

Chad shoved the newcomer away.

"Do *not* call me kiddo!" Chad said.

Jake looked to Raven. "Things did not end well between us," he admitted.

"You don't say," she said.

"*This* is when you decide to start telling people about us?" Chad demanded. He towered over Raven. His manicured fingernails grew into sharp claws.

"Where's Troy?" he growled.

Raven touched her jaw gingerly. Not broken—some good news amidst this cluster bomb. She glared at Jake. Damn exes, budding in when they ought to be running.

"Get out of here," she said to Jake. "You don't know what you're doing. He's dangerous."

"Come on," Jake said, pulling Chad away from her.

"I can take her," Chad said, puffing his muscular chest.

Jake gripped Chad's arm. "She's not alone. I've seen what they can do. You're going to lose."

"That is so like you," Chad snapped. "Why can't you ever be supportive?"

Raven curled her fingers into fists. From the store's rear exit came Pixie and Desirée, armed with tranquilizer guns. The phony paramedic returned through the front of the store.

"Where's Troy?" Chad barked at her.

The paramedic held a rifle that looked like it fired a net.

"Step away from him," Raven said to Jake.

"You heard her," Chad said, "step away."

"Chad, do you trust me?" Jake asked.

"Girl, please," he snapped. "You dumped me! I will *never* trust you."

"That's fair, but…" Jake's words trailed off as he yanked Chad into his body and hugged him tight. Darts and a weighted net flew at them, too much for even Chad to avoid. Raven smiled. The little turd was about to get his due.

Yet, as the projectiles closed in on their target, Raven's smile turned brittle. "What the…?"

She shielded her eyes against a growing swirl of lavender-pink light. At first, she thought it was the store's fluorescents reacting to a power surge. She cursed as she realized the light was coming from Jake's physique. It exploded out of his form, wrapped around him and Chad, and hid them within cotton candy swirls of incandescence. The currents of energy pulled inwards, imploding in purple and pink sparks.

The darts smacked and quivered in the wall. Half of the net landed atop of Diesel's unconscious form. The Aberbombie manager lay upon a fallen male dummy, lips to lips. The other half of the net was gone—so were Chad and Jake.

"Mother of Christ," Raven swore.

"The Judeo-Christian faith has subjugated women around the world," Pixie chastised. "You shouldn't invoke Marie's name."

"A teleporter," Raven snorted. "We've got a bloody teleporter to deal with."

And that muscle twink had made a fool of her. Her jaw jutted as she shoved Diesel aside and crushed the face of the fallen Aberbombie dummy with her boot.

She planned on doing far worse to Chad when she got her hands on him.

Chapter 6

Troy Allstar stood before a gravestone, his yellow A&S track pants flapping about his legs in the steady wind. The sky was grey; the air chilled his bare pecs and feet.

Are you able to feel cold in a dream? he wondered.

He knew this wasn't real. The details were wrong. What ought to have been a simple gravestone was a towering angel; it belonged in the middle of a cemetery, not next to a dilapidated country church on top of a hill.

Jesse Truesdale was etched into the stone at the winged statue's feet. In the real world, it also read, *Beloved Son and Brother.* The epitaph in this dreamscape reflected the one burned into Troy's heart. His throat constricted as he read it aloud, "Troy Allstar's Bestest Bud and Truest Love."

Jesse killed himself after a pair of super-powered teens hell-bent on destroying Nuffim High outed him.

If I'd been there for him, been a better friend, maybe more than a friend...

Troy wiped tears from his eyes. The emotions were all mixed up with each other. He loved Chad, felt it in his chest every time he thought about the cheerleader; holding him and being held by him always made the world brighter. Troy missed Jesse for what they were and for what they might have been. Troy's connection with Jesse went deeper than his heart.

I could feel him in my bones, Troy thought. *We were soulmates.* How could Chad ever compete with that?

"It's not a competition," a familiar voice said from behind him.

Troy turned.

Jesse? he thought—but no; the details were off.

"Hello, Felix," Troy said to Jesse's older brother.

"We don't have much time," Felix said.

"We never do," Troy agreed. He looked down. He held the Paris Hilton journal. The heiress' face was slashed with deep claw marks and spattered with blood. Etched into the cover were the words, *I warned you.*

Felix's hand settled on Troy's shoulder.

"They've come," Troy said.

"Yes," Felix replied. "Now we have to fight back."

How? was the question on Troy's lips, but it never emerged. There was something about Felix that nagged at him. Troy reached out and caressed the taller youth's cheeks. He was warm to the touch.

"You're real," Troy said with wonder, his empathic powers sensing that this was not some conjured image from his mind. Felix was here, in Troy's dream.

"How?" Troy pressed.

"I'm not sure," Felix admitted. "I'm a telepath, but dreams run too deep for me to reach. The others are nearby."

"Others?" Troy asked, fearing Felix was talking about Chad, Gibbie, and Mandy.

"Friends of mine," Felix said. "Those women captured us..."

Troy caught flashes of their attackers around the gravestone—the redhead with her wildly curly hair, Raven and her biceps from a fitness magazine, and the other two, toughs Desirée and Chantal.

"...they've drugged me, I think," Felix continued. "But you, somehow, I can reach you."

Troy nodded as if mind reading and dream sharing were the most normal things in the world. He looked at the angel on the gravestone. It had been replaced by Chad. He stood there, frozen, hands pressed together in prayer, radiant in a pair of silver Speedos, a manifestation of Troy's subconscious.

"I'll keep you safe," Troy promised him.

Without realizing it, he reached over to grasp Felix's hand. It was solid and sure—reassuring in a world where everything had turned to chaos.

Meanwhile, as Troy dreamed a not-so-little dream, outside Nuffim Mall, Raven sat in the driver's seat of an ambulance. She jerked the steering wheel, and the squeal of tires split the air as the vehicle turned at a sharp angle. The parking lot was a madhouse, but the sound of police sirens was yet to be heard.

Good, Raven thought. No cops meant Pixie's tech performed to spec, scrambling any 9-11 calls—for now. Their hack job also immobilized any attempts to grab cell-phone video of tonight's events. The security cameras had been dealt with on site, with phony video implanted of masked men robbing the mall's jewelry store. Let the cops think this was a heist. There'd be eyewitnesses, but with the fake video, who was to say what happened?

Technologically, tonight's raid had been flawless, but everything else had turned into a pig roast. Raven glanced into the rear of the ambulance. Troy Allstar, the one they'd codenamed Romeo, was thrashing atop a gurney. They'd cut his shirt and taped medical electrodes all over his etched torso, feeding a slew of readings into a laptop. His eyes popped open, and his back arched.

"Felix?" he cried, gazing about blindly.

"Sedate him!" Raven shouted.

"He *is* sedated!" Desirée bellowed. A heart monitor bleeped in staccato bursts. "The drugs aren't working! I think he's going into cardiac arrest!"

"You *think*?" Raven demanded.

"I have basic CPR," Desirée blurted. She gestured at her paramedic outfit. "I'm wearing a costume, not a uniform!"

Useless! Raven raged. *Do I have to do everything?*

The sound of sirens split the air. *Crap!* Her heart rate spiked at the thought of police cornering them, demanding answers she didn't have, then running her ID—a flawless fake—unless it wasn't. Her breathing quickened. What if they found out her true identity? The dishonorable discharge despite her Purple Hearts? She tasted blood as she bit the inside of her cheek.

Even in her fear, she habitually checked her rearview mirror like she'd learned as a teenager from her Gestapo driving instructor—also known as Dad. She spotted a spindly figure in the distance—and something else. A shadow chased the ambulance, overtaking it as they approached the exit from the parking lot. The undulating black silhouette reminded Raven of the shadows cast by fighter jets.

But the town of Nuffim had no airfield, and this shade possessed no wings.

Raven craned her neck over the dash—a blazing firebird glared down at her from an orange sports car sailing through the air. Its front bumper smashed into the ground in front of her with a deafening crash. The hood crumpled; the car teetered and toppled.

Raven slammed the brakes; the ambulance careened to a halt in front of the ravaged vehicle.

"Effing hell!" Desirée cursed from behind her.

Raven rammed the gear into reverse. The engine growled, the tires revved, but the ambulance didn't budge. The smell of burning rubber filled the air, followed by a loud pop. In the side mirror, Raven saw a wheel and hubcap go flying.

The one named Gibbie, whom they'd codenamed Bully, held up the back of the van. He kicked the other back tire; it, too, went flying. He dropped the van, throwing Raven up then back into her seat.

She shook her head as Gibbie walked around the vehicle. His fingers crunched into the metal of the van's sliding door, ripping it off as if he were pulling tissue from a box. Raven was still awed by what these brats could do. Gibbie tossed the door aside. He grabbed Desirée, yanked her out of the vehicle, and dismissively threw her impressive frame a dozen feet to his right. She landed with a grunt and a crunch of metal, caving in the roof of a Volvo.

Gibbie climbed inside and stared down Raven, right into the barrel of the gun she didn't recall drawing. It wasn't a Taser or loaded with drugged darts. It was the real deal, with real bullets.

"Leave my brother alone," Gibbie said.

His voice cracked half-way through the sentence, adding to the ridiculousness of the scene. He was a waif, especially compared to Troy's buffed physique, but here it was, the world flipped upside down, the little nerd come to rescue his jock brother who lay helpless and unconscious.

Raven fired.

Elsewhere, in a place between spaces, Chad was aware of warmth and a sense of safety—as if he were snuggled in a womb, protected and oblivious to all that life could throw his way. Then, with violent indifference, a thousand hooks pierced his skin, violently tossing him into a cold void filled with spiraling razor blades.

Vertigo wrenched him, and he landed instinctively on all fours. Half of a net flopped like a dying fish next to him, its ends fried and sizzling.

"Home sweet home," Jake said, his handsome brow beaded with sweat. His arm tattoo glistened in the dappled moonlight coming from a window.

They were no longer in Aberbombie and Stitch. Whatever Jake had done, it had taken them several blocks away. Chad recognized the posters of Axel Rose, the worn mahogany desk that once belonged to Jake's grandfather, a twin bed, covered in a flannel grey cover, and a Quran on the bedside table, no doubt put there by Jake's mom.

Chad stood and banged his head on the sloped ceiling of Jake's attic bedroom.

"Just like old times," Jake said.

Chad gave him cut-eye. How many nights had Chad dreamt of being here again, in Jake's bedroom *and* in his arms?

"We're fleeing psychos and *this* is where you bring me?" Chad demanded.

"I can only teleport to places I've been, and…I don't know, this felt safe," Jake explained.

"Take me back," Chad ordered.

"Are you crazy?" Jake said.

"I'm not leaving Troy behind," Chad snapped.

Jake flinched.

"Those women, they're dangerous," Jake said. "Didn't you get my warning?"

"The journal," Chad realized. "It was you who wrote that message."

Before Jake could reply, Chad's phone rang. A picture of Troy and Chad appeared on the display. Chad answered with relief. Troy must've gotten away.

"Excuse me," Chad said, putting the phone to his ear. "It's my boyfriend."

Jake turned to the round window. In the distance, lights from emergency vehicles flashed in the Nuffim Mall parking lot.

"Troy?" Chad said, moving about the room. "Troy, can you hear me?" To Jake, Chad asked, "Has your reception always been this bad in here?"

"Maybe he butt-dialed you," Jake said. "Maybe he's not as worried about you as you are about…"

Jake's words trailed off. A black Hummer pulled onto the lawn. A petite redhead got out, carrying a rifle. She was followed by a woman in sunglasses atop a nose that had clearly been broken on more than one occasion.

"Crap," Jake said, wondering how the hell they'd gotten here so fast.

"Can you hear me now?" Chad asked. "Troy?"

Chad climbed onto a desk, his head enshrined by a skylight.

"Damn it!" Jake said, grabbing Chad's arm.

He fell atop of Jake, their frames pressed firmly together on the floor.

"Rude!" Chad said.

Stamping feet grew louder, coming up the stairs. Chad's pointed ears twitched, his nostrils flared, and a low whine built in his throat. He hissed as the door flew open. The red head fired a pair of tranquilizer guns.

Jake grabbed the front of Chad's jeans. Chad saw the net cut in half by the previous teleport and pressed tightly against Jake as purple-pink light flared around them.

Chapter 7

In an ambulance outside Nuffim Mall, Raven felt her finger pull the trigger of the gun aimed at Gibbie. She heard the boom as she fired. She would've done anything to take that bullet back. The mission was capture, not execute, but in the heat of the moment, she'd gone into survival mode—kill or be killed. But was that all, or was her wounded ego out for blood?

He's better off put down, her inner voice assured her.

It was a clean shot with only one possible outcome. It would blast through the kid's forehead and blow out the back of his skull, sending bits of bone and brain in an outward spray. She was supposed to be sticking up for dweebs like this, turning him into someone who could stick up for himself without becoming a grade-A douche in the process. Instead, this is what she'd become —a child killer. That's what that devil had done to her.

All this flashed through her mind as that singular instant became torturously slow. Within that time lapse came another impossibility; a buzzing shield of blue energy popped up around Gibbie as a young woman appeared from nowhere. The bullet bounced off the shield, leaving a hole in the ceiling of the ambulance.

"Drop it," the teen ordered, giving a sassy flip or her black hair.

Raven recognized her. She was friends with the clan of juiced gay boys. Her names was Sandy or Blandy or…Mandy? But that blue shield, what was that? Was it coming from her?

A girl with powers! How?

They'd thought only gay boys could get these crazy abilities. The Etienne water had done nothing for Raven or her companions when they'd tried it. That's when it clicked.

Straight girl. The water transforms gay boys and straight girls. That must be it. Raven held the gun steady. Sweat poured from Mandy's forehead. "Must be exhausting keeping that forcefield going," Raven said with mock sympathy.

Gibbie, looked worried. "Mandy—" he began.

"I got this," Mandy snapped. Her shield flickered in disagreement.

"Don't think you can hold it for much longer," Raven taunted.

Mandy shrugged. "Don't need to." She pressed the shield against Raven's gun; a jolt of energy sent the weapon flying out of Raven's hand. It cracked the windshield and clanked onto the floor. Raven grabbed it, but it fell from her numbed fingers. Mandy's shield fizzled away, confirming Raven's suspicion. She'd run out of steam.

"Sorry about your hand," the girl said.

"I've got another one," Raven replied, diving at the girl.

"Gibbie!" Mandy shrieked, dropping with the speed and grace of a cheerleading trophy winner.

Gibbie palmed Raven's chest. It looked like a gentle tap, yet she flew back with such force she smashed through the windshield, shattering it into a kaleidoscope of glass. She sailed over the hood and landed against the pavement, knocking the wind from her. She tried to inhale—nothing—then air slammed into her. The breath was delicious agony.

Get up Raven, she ordered herself.

She tasted iron and spit blood. She imagined what she looked like—barely able to stand, clothes battered and ripped, lip puffy and bleeding. She staggered like a zombie from *Dawn of the Lesbian Dead*.

Her phone was on the ground, the screen cracked. A message beeped from Pixie. *Cornering Feline and the new guy. I think we should call him Trick. Get it? Because he's in and out* 😏.

Gibbie stepped out of the ambulance, cradling his brother in his arms. Mandy put a reassuring hand on Gibbie's shoulder and met Raven's eye. Raven blinked, and the three teenagers were gone—all except for Mandy's tongue, which hovered there, attached to nothing, sticking out and mocking.

"What the…" Raven began.

As if in response, the tongue curled back and vanished.

Miles away, along the highway to Nuffim, stood a local gem named Mom and Pop's Café. It was known for its amazing sweet potato fries, homemade aioli, and freshly baked pies. The front of the diner was a silver camper with smooth curves and rounded mariner windows. A *CLOSED* sign was hanging inside the main door. Outside, a billboard displayed two grinning children eating sundaes. Street artists had given them devil horns.

Pink light flared from behind the restaurant's shuttered vinyl blinds.

Inside, the bubblegum luminescence washed over a poster of a woman in blue overalls, her hair held back by a red kerchief with white polka dots, flexing her arm and boasting, *WE CAN DO IT!*

The deserted counter was a polished blue melamine that harkened back to yesteryear. Swivel stools of chrome and bright yellow sat empty, and the chalkboard declared, *MILKSHAKE SPECIAL with every burger and fries!*

The purple-pink light bled away. In its wake, it left two hunks lying on top of the counter. Jake's fingers clung to the front of Chad's pants. He looked around. "You have got to be kidding me," he said. "Mom and Pop's Café? Seriously?"

He shoved himself from Jake and nimbly landed on the floor.

"Your cell phone," Jake said. "That's how they found us."

Chad stared at it in his hand and quickly powered it down. Was that enough? Should he wrap it in tinfoil? Did that make a difference?

Jake shakily got to his feet.

"Enough of this trip down memory lane. Take me back to the mall, *now*," Chad ordered.

"Yeah, sure," Jake panted. "Just need to catch my…"

His words slurred; his eyes rolled back; his body convulsed. He twirled clumsily and stumbled into the counter, grabbing at it as his knees gave out.

"Jake!" Chad cried, catching his ex before he could slam into the linoleum floor. Jake shook. "Sugar," he wheezed.

"Do *not* call me sug—" Chad started to say. Jake pointed desperately at the ice cream freezer.

"Oh," Chad said. "Right."

Chad hopped over and scooped a ball of rocky road onto a cone and came back, handing it to Jake.

"My favorite," he said, his eyes fluttering in ecstasy as he consumed it like a starving man. "You remembered."

"Less talking, more licking," Chad snapped. Jake raised an eyebrow, clearly intrigued by the suggestion.

"Don't," Chad warned.

Jake shrugged, finishing off the cone.

"Teleporting burns a lot of calories. I usually keep chocolate bars on me," Jake said.

"That sounds like a Jake problem," Chad replied.

"How are you *more* sensitive than I remember?" Jake said.

Chad's hackles rose; with an effort, he forced them down. "I'm not playing that game. It's tired. Are you taking me back to Troy or what?"

"Yeah," Jake said. "I owe you that much."

"That doesn't cover the interest on what you owe me," Chad said.

Jake held out his hand. After a moment of hesitation, Chad took it. The smallest of lumps formed in his throat as he stared into his ex's hazel brown eyes.

"In case something bad happens when we go back, there's something I want you to know," Jake said. "That time we came here, I liked it—way more than I was willing to admit. It was…special. Anyway, thanks for the rocky road."

Before Chad could answer, Jake squeezed his ex's fingers, purple-pink light swirled around them, and they were gone.

Troy stared at the cinder block walls of a compact cell. It had a steel pan for a toilet, a narrow cot, and an iron door locked from the other side. He wore a baby blue wrestling singlet. The fabric was worn about the thighs, and the swooping neckline seemed designed to show off his pecs, nipples poking out on either side. He'd tossed this singlet years ago. It's how he knew this was another dream.

"You made it," Felix said with relief. "I was worried you wouldn't be back."

Troy turned and faced Jesse's older brother.

"Is this where they're holding you?" Troy asked, taking in the older youth's broad shoulders, dressed in orange prison overalls. He looked so much like Jesse, it both hurt and felt good.

Felix nodded. "I even know where here is—kind of. Blake was coming to when they brought him in the back of the pickup. The tarp on him blew off. He saw the outside of this place, and I saw what he saw."

"Can you show me?" Troy asked.

"In a dream?" Felix asked. "I don't know. I usually can't reach people's dreams. But you're different."

"Maybe we're different together," Troy replied. "Try."

Felix closed his eyes; nothing happened. Felix looked to Troy in frustration. "It's not working."

"Maybe we need a stronger link," Troy offered. He had an idea how to make that happen—one that Chad would not let him live down if he ever found out.

Troy took Felix's hand. It was solid and real, as real as if they were physically standing together. The contact sent a rush of goosebumps up Troy's bare arm.

"Try again," Troy said.

"I…Okay," Felix said.

The walls flickered, then turned solid once more.

"You're holding back," Troy said. "I can sense it."

"It's just, this feels so—" Felix stammered.

"Intimate," Troy finished for him. If he ever told Chad about this, Troy thought it best to leave that word out. "We're sharing a dream. This *is* intimate. Maybe that's the key."

"I'm taken," Felix said, "and you're thinking things you shouldn't be thinking, about me, about…"

"I'm also taken," Troy interrupted, clasping Felix's unresisting fingers before he could mention Jesse by name, "and you're feeling things you shouldn't be feeling. Do you want to be rescued?"

"I do," Felix said.

"Let's do what we need to do, think what we need to think, feel what we need to feel, to get you and your boyfriend out of here, and no more, yeah?"

"Yeah. No more," Felix agreed.

"Show me what Blake saw," Troy told him.

Again the walls flickered, revealing trees beyond.

"It's working," Troy said, pushing Chad from his mind. "Stand closer."

Felix looked to the ceiling. "Forgive me," he whispered.

"For your boyfriend," Troy said.

"For Alejandro," Felix agreed.

They stepped together. Their bodies touched. The outside world grew stronger, but not enough for Troy to figure out where Felix was being held. Troy slid his hand around Felix's waist. In the real world, Troy was a master of restraint, but here, his subconscious ran the show. There was so much he repressed with Jesse; Felix made Troy feel like this was a second chance.

"Only what's necessary," Felix said, wrapping his hand around Troy's waist.

"No more, no less," Troy agreed, breathing heavily.

Trees and fields formed around them.

Troy hugged Felix. Felix hugged back, the breath of one growing ragged in the ear of the other.

Troy kissed Felix—one kiss, in the crook of the neck. It didn't have to mean anything. It was part of the mission.

"It's the only way to strengthen our link, to get us out of here," Felix agreed, reading Troy's mind. He kissed Troy's neck in return.

The walls of Felix's prison dissolved. There it was—a sign, with the name of the farm where Felix was being held.

"Only what's necessary," Troy said, wanting so much more.

"Only what's necessary," Felix agreed, holding Troy back with a hand on his chest.

"I'm coming for you…" Troy said, about to call Felix by his brother's name. Troy caught himself, but it didn't matter, not with a telepath.

Felix patted Troy's hand kindly.

"I know you are," Felix replied and shoved Troy away.

As Felix and Troy barely resisted temptation, Mandy and Gibbie hunkered down in Gibbie's bedroom.

Mandy was perched over Gibbie's desk, fingers parting the horizontal blinds so she could keep a lookout in case those madwomen followed them here. A motorcycle pulled to a stop in the driveway. Chad was on the back, but who was driving? Mandy leaned closer to the window.

"Careful of my—" Gibbie began.

"*Battlestar Galactica* model Viper," Mandy interrupted.

"It's signed by—" Gibbie began defensively.

"Katie Sackhoff," Mandy piped in. "Chad's here. You should let him in."

"He's got a key," Gibbie answered.

Since when? Mandy wanted to ask. She rolled her eyes, figuring it out. "Of course he does."

Gibbie glanced at his older brother, curled on Gibbie's bed and clutching a stuffed baby Yoda.

"We're in here!" Gibbie's voice squeaked as Chad bounded up the stairs.

Chad rushed in, dropped to Troy's side, and took his hand. "Is he okay? Are you guys? We tried going to the mall, but the police said they sent everyone home."

Chad looked at them long enough to confirm no one was missing any limbs —then all his attention was back on Troy. Mandy took note.

Thankfully, a new target for her pissy mood shifted sheepishly in the doorway. The mysterious motorcycle driver stood revealed, helmet in one hand, broad shoulders forming a shelf for his sleeveless shirt, and faux-diamond earrings glittering in the light.

The edge in Mandy's voice made him flinch.

"Jake—"

"Kanaan," Gibbie finished for her. His eyes were wide with worship.

"Hey," Jake said.

Gibbie looked hurriedly about the room, but though his super strength made him the fastest runner in the world, it was too late to hide his collection of Dalek figurines, a *Dungeons & Dragons* chess set, and an under-construction floor-to-ceiling Lego space station.

"That's not mine," Gibbie lied. "This is Troy's room."

"Gibbie, you can do better than this turd with legs," Mandy said. "Just ask Chad."

"You guys dated?" Gibbie said with a combination of wonder, jealousy, and hope. "Jake, you're into guys?"

"Thanks for giving Chad a ride from the mall, Kanaan. Now you can go," Mandy said.

"I don't think I can," Jake replied. He closed the door, staying in the room.

"He's one of us," Chad said before Mandy could object.

"He's one of—" Mandy began.

"He's got powers," Chad clarified. "He's the one who wrote the warning in my journal."

"That was you?" Mandy asked.

Jake shrugged in an 'it was the least I could do' kind of way. "You're welcome."

"You wrote a childish note in a Paris Hilton diary when you knew those freaks were out there, ready to come and get us?" Mandy snapped. "That's psychotic."

Jake blushed, the crimson glow spreading from his cheeks to the exposed tops of his pecs. "It's...complicated."

"It's what now?" Mandy sputtered. "This is not your twisted social media relationship status. These are our lives. Do you get that? We could've been killed."

"I tried," Jake said.

"You tried what?" Mandy snapped. "To call? To text? To email?"

"Yes," Jake said. "I tried it all. I tried driving into town. I tried writing a regular letter for eff's sake. And every time I did, every time I picked up the phone or tried to press send, or I got behind the wheel, I teleported somewhere else. I even teleported into Chad's room, and as soon as I saw him get home from school, my power revved up, and I grabbed the first thing I could."

"The journal," Chad explained.

"So your superpower is turning into a chickenshit?" Mandy said, holding her finger towards Chad to stop him from talking. Her glare focused on Jake as if she were a reality-show judge about to say, "Sashay away."

"You think I haven't beaten myself up already?" Jake yelled.

"I don't see any bruises," she snapped.

"Fine. You want to blame me, blame me. As far as I'm concerned, I was smart. I kept it cryptic, tricked my subconscious, or whatever part of me controls this power, into not freaking out, to not panic at the thought of seeing the guy I love..."

That raised everyone's eyebrows.

"I mean loved..."

Second sets of eyebrows raised.

"I mean liked..."

Heads tilted to one side, appraising this statement as well.

"I mean," Jake continued to sputter, "someone I considered a friendly person to spend time with outside of school when, you know, I wasn't busy, with stuff, like football, and things, and, sure, when I was feeling horned up. There, you happy now? Is that what you want to hear?"

Jake wiped the sweat forming on his brow then looked at his hand. It pulsed with a lavender light. "Oh, crap."

"Ditching us so soon?" Mandy asked in a 'what are you still doing here?' kind of way.

"I think it's a fight or flight response," Jake said, the veins standing out on his biceps. The purple glow grew brighter; pink sparks danced off of him.

"You teleport," Mandy said. "That makes it a flight or flight response."

Jake ignored her, closing his eyes. "I'm in my happy place, I'm in my happy place..." he murmured over and over, his pecs widening and contracting as he took slow, deep breaths.

Gibbie held up his phone and took a photo. "I think I'm in my happy place too."

The energy pulsing from Jake faded, came back, faded again, as if trying to decide what to do.

"Let me help," Mandy said. She touched his shirt and pants with her pointing finger and thumb. Smirking, she made his clothes turn invisible.

His eyes widened, catching sight of his fully exposed muscle bod in the mirror. He covered his crotch, hands pressed between his thick, smooth thighs.

The purple-pink energy flared, wrapping around him. Chad jerked Mandy back, and, in a whoosh of imploding light, Jake was gone.

"I thought he'd never shut up," Mandy said, pulling out her compact and touching up her lipstick.

"Mandy, if you'd been caught in his wake, he could've taken your arm off," Chad said, recalling what had happened to the net their attackers fired at him.

"Like, actually?" she asked.

"Hey there," a drowsy Troy interrupted.

All eyes turned to the fallen wrestler, snuggled with baby Yoda. Mandy snapped her compact closed.

"Troy?" Chad called, his eyes tearing up. "Can you hear me? It's Chad!"

"Felix," Troy murmured in his sleep.

"Did he say Felix?" Chad said.

"He's been going in and out like that for a while," Mandy said. "Don't worry; he'll be okay."

"You don't know," Chad snapped, making Gibbie wince.

"Duh," Mandy countered. "My mom's a nurse."

"Oh, right," Chad agreed.

Troy's body convulsed, thrashing from side to side. Mandy stopped preening, pointing her nail file at Troy. "That's new."

Gibbie was about to hold his brother down when Troy sucked in his breath and sat upright, gasping, his bare torso dripping with sweat. His eyes roved wildly.

"Troy? Troy!" Chad called. Troy stared aimlessly, lungs fighting for air.

He pressed his back against the wall as if being cornered.

"It's okay; it's me!" Chad said.

"Boo bear?" Troy asked.

"I'm going to vomit and not because of my eating disorder, which is under control, by the way, thank for you not bothering to ask or care," Mandy said.

"I asked you how your group was going," Gibbie interjected.

"Shhh," Mandy said. "I'm causing a scene."

"It's okay," Chad told his boyfriend, "you're safe."

"Felix!" Troy cried, looking around the room as if searching for the most important person in the world.

"And this Felix person is?" Chad said, an edge creeping into his voice.

"Trouble in Club Paradise?" Mandy asked hopefully.

Troy shook his head, clearing his mind. He placed a comforting hand on top of Chad's.

"Relax," Troy said. He'd barely woken up, and already he was going into comforting Chad mode.

Chad waited for the usual sense of ease to settle in. It was easy to do when Troy was around, speaking like that, his voice calm and soothing, taking him to a place of serenity. Chad waited. And waited. Then waited a bit more. That sense of lounging on the beach didn't come. Troy's words, usually a balm, felt like a skipping stone that sinks instead of skimming artfully across the water. It was almost as if Troy's attention were somewhere else—or on someone else.

"Who's Felix?" Chad pressed.

"He's Jesse's brother," Troy panted—probably because he'd woken up from a drugged stupor after being kidnapped. Yet, he spoke of Felix the way Chad would talk about the latest top 40s pop queen—with reverence.

"Are you okay?" Gibbie asked Chad, easily holding him back.

Stop being a spaz, Chad told himself, willing his claws to recede. "I'm fine."

"Felix is like us," Troy explained. "He can do things. Come to think of it, maybe he was the one who wrote in my Paris Hilton journal."

Chad exchanged a guilty glance with Mandy.

"About that..." Chad began, not sure how to explain that it was, in fact, his ex who'd written the warning, and who'd been teleporting Chad all about town, including into Jake's bedroom.

"Yes, Chad," Mandy said, folding her arms over her chest, "do elaborate."

Nothing happened, Chad assured himself. So why the lingering sense of guilt, which Troy was going to sense with his damn powers and completely misinterpret? "There's something I should tell you—" Chad began, but Troy wasn't paying attention to Chad's feelings or words.

"Those women," Troy cut him off.

That's fine, he's in problem-solving mode. I like that he's a take-charge kind of guy, Chad assured himself.

"Chad!" Gibbie demanded. "What are you doing to baby Yoda?"

Chad's claws dug into the plush toy's head.

"Those women have Felix and his friends," Troy said. "We're going to bust them out."

Chapter 8

In a second-floor bedroom in a secluded farmhouse on the outskirts of Nuffim, Raven slammed open the double doors of a floor-to-ceiling cabinet, revealing an arsenal that would make a weapons dealer squeal.

"Well, that was a pig roast," Raven said to the handguns, rifles, and Uzis neatly arranged alongside a range of knives, throwing stars, nunchucks, grenades, Tasers, and a bazooka.

Hanging on the opposite wall was an oil painting of a decolonized, Indigenized, and queerified representation of reconciliation in the forms of the goddesses Artemis and Pinga. The pair ravished each other atop a bed of slain polar bears, walrus, and narwhal. The beasts oozed blood from the arrows, spears, and harpoons penetrating their hides.

"Not our smoothest operation," Pixie agreed as Raven stripped herself of the daggers strapped to her thighs, the gun at her waist, the Taser tucked into a holster at her hip, a police club, and a canister of rubber bullets. She winced and hissed, her body a criss-cross of cuts and lacerations. She looked like she'd stepped out of Tim Burton's *The Nightmare Before Queermas*. Using tweezers, she pulled glass from various parts of her body.

"I almost shot that kid in the face," Raven barked.

"But you didn't," Pixie said, drawing up the sleeves of her lab coat. Underneath she wore a simple orange T-shirt and blue jeans. The metallic black stone around her throat glittered in the light of an antique lamp.

She hunched over an artfully distressed mahogany desk. Lush curtains draped to the floor's rough wood planks; a colorful quilt and a mountain of knitted pillows drowned a four-poster bed. The décor was lavish compared to the barracks Raven was used to.

This doesn't make me soft, she assured herself. *You better be right,* another part of her answered. Her gaze brought that point home, locking onto a thick steel door. It looked like it belonged on a bank vault with its massive hinges and a multitude of locking mechanisms. It was stamped *WEAPON XY* in big steel letters.

"Did you at least get some useful data out of this piss storm?" Raven asked, pulling her gaze away from the vault door. She stripped out of her military wear —caked with dried blood—and began disinfecting her wounds.

"Muriel, display data from subjects Romeo and Know-It-All," Pixie said.

A three-dimensional holographic projection sprung to life above the antique desk, showing images of Troy and Felix, along with a slew of data, charting brainwaves, heartbeats, and testicular function. Pixie was thorough with her scans.

"Thank you Muriel," Pixie said, speaking to the computer as if it were a living thing.

"*Anything else ma'am?*" its mechanically sultry voice echoed.

"Oh, you don't have to call me ma'am," Pixie said.

"*Yes ma'am,*" Muriel replied with a wink-wink tone.

It was an old glitch and an old joke, which Raven had little patience for as she stitched herself. "Containing them didn't work. Maybe I should've shot that kid," Raven said half-heartedly. She looked at her arsenal on the wall, then at the steel door marked *WEAPON XY*.

"We're not executioners," Pixie said, flipping through the holographic information.

"I wasn't—"

"Weren't you?" Pixie said, following Raven's stare to the vault door. "We have to be better. Where's the focusing stone I gave you?"

Raven fished in her pocket and pulled out a black orb that matched the one around Pixie's neck. She set it on the desk and sat next to it, her backside blurring some of the projected data. Pixie resumed sorting through the 3-D files.

"Do you care that we've blown our cover," Raven vented, "that those freaks are running about wild, and that girl—"

Pixie stopped throwing around holographic readings at the mention of Mandy.

"Yes. The girl. She has powers."

"The *straight* girl," Raven emphasized.

"The Etienne water doesn't work on dykes," Pixie concluded, "but it does on heterosexual females and gay males."

"Once again, the lesbians get screwed," Raven sulked, pacing in front of the steel vault.

"Not if I have my way," the spritely redhead said.

She returned to her graphs and readings.

"There you are," Pixie said, as if pulling a willful cat from under the couch. She enlarged one particular set of data. Raven assessed the series of lines spiking up and down.

"Brain scans?" she asked.

"Correct," Pixie replied, smiling broadly.

Raven came to her side, intrigued.

"Do you see it?" Pixie asked.

What am I missing? Raven wondered, afraid of looking dumb. She gazed at the glowing lines. From the corner of her eye, something else screamed for her attention—a dark shape flying towards the window. It grew larger. Raven turned towards it, eyes widening.

She grabbed Pixie, shielding her body as she dove them into the hall a second before their Mad Max Hummer smashed through the window. The black vehicle obliterated the mahogany desk. The hologram winked out.

"*Proximity alert,*" Muriel's electronic voice informed them.

"Better never than late!" Raven yelled at the computer, simultaneously looking to the steel door with the words *WEAPON XY*. It remained secure; one blessing at least. Her hand went for her gun, but she was unarmed. She stared across the room at her cache of weapons on the other side of the Hummer. She pushed herself to her feet and sprinted for the cabinet; before taking two steps, something swept her legs out from under her.

She caught sight of Chad. She kicked at where he'd stood a moment ago; her foot found only empty air.

How can anyone move so fast?

Her answer came in the form of a fist smashing her in the side of the face so hard she spun around and landed palms to the floor. Pain shot up her knees and into her spine, but she barely noticed as the room swam before her. She tasted blood, dripping from her nose to her lips.

Woman up, Raven, her inner drill sergeant commanded, but it was hard to obey. The room blurred. She was fading.

"That's it," she heard the one called Troy say. "You're feeling more and more tired. Feeling heavy. So very heavy."

Her arms gave out from under her, and she sprawled on the floor. Next to her was Pixie, out cold. A few feet away was Pixie's necklace with the metallic stone. Raven struggled towards it, but her body seemed impossibly heavy.

Fight it! Raven ordered herself, crawling closer.

Drowsily, she watched Gibbie jump to the second story and land inside the gaping hole in the wall, Mandy cradled in his arms.

"Sleep," Troy said again.

Raven tried to stare him down, but her eyelids were so heavy, she *wanted* to sleep. Her fingers closed around the black stone. The weight of Troy's empathic powers didn't disappear, but it cut significantly. It was enough. She smiled victoriously. Her grip tightened into a fist.

"Lady, my boyfriend said sleep," Chad snapped at her.

She felt his arms squeeze around her neck restricting her oxygen supply. Her grip on the stone relaxed; her eyes fluttered shut.

The last thing she saw was the steel door labeled *WEAPON XY.*

Chad dropped Raven's limp form. Her head smacked against the carpeted floor.

"Chad!" Mandy said as Gibbie set her down.

"What?" Chad replied. "She had it coming."

"I could've Boomeranged her head bounce," Mandy replied.

"Come on. There's still two of them," Troy said.

Chad sniffed the air and tilted his head, his pointed ears catching the sound of their foes' running feet.

"Positions," Troy said.

When Chantal and Desirée burst through the door, they gaped at the Hummer in the room, tilted at an angle, wheels still turning. They both wore overalls covered in grease. They leveled their weapons at Troy, Mandy, and Chad, then fired a net and a slew of darts, all of which bounced off Mandy's shield. Gibbie slid in behind them, reached up, and knocked their heads together.

"*Three Stooges* style," Gibbie said as they fell.

"Got it!" Mandy said, recording the whole thing on her phone.

"Come on!" Troy said, jumping over the fallen women.

"Yeah, guys, stop fooling around," Chad agreed, waiting for Troy to approve of his support, but Troy was gone from sight.

Chad hurried after him down a cheery yellow hallway. Framed prints of herb sketches decorated the walls. He passed the open door of a bedroom. Dangling Edison bulbs sprayed light onto a bed frame made from metal cogs, a pressure-powered clock ticking on the wall, and an old-school typewriter on a desk refurbished from a sewing machine stand. It reminded Chad of Gibbie's love for steampunk. How dare these women have anything in common with Gibbie? It gave them an air of humanity they didn't deserve.

"Felix?" Troy shouted, spinning like a compass seeking true north.

Chad's nostrils flared. "I can smell them, they're—"

"In the basement," Troy yelled, bounding down the stairs two at a time.

Chad loped on his heels, eyes ears, and nose scanning for any danger to Troy, ready to defend him to the death. But there weren't any threats for Chad to fight—none that he could see, hear, or smell. They reached the door to basement and down the pair went, followed by Mandy and Gibbie.

While the old farmhouse's current occupants had retained much of the building's original charm, the same could not be said about the cellar.

Chad watched his head under the low ceiling and stared down a narrow concrete corridor. Industrial light fixtures flickered on the walls. Several steel doors were closed and appeared locked.

"They must've built this themselves," Chad shivered—not from the damp air alone.

"Guantanamo meets Home Depot," Mandy agreed from over his shoulder.

"There!" Troy pointed at one of the closed doors. The others followed, hurrying past several unoccupied rooms, doors open, each with a small cot, a bedpan in the corner, and not much else.

These were meant for us, Chad realized.

"Creepy," Gibbie said.

"He's in here!" Troy shouted, pulling, then banging on an unyielding door. "Felix? Felix! Can you hear me? Gibbie, get over here!"

Gibbie cracked his knuckles and yanked the door off its hinges. Troy rushed in and dropped to his knees next to Felix, who was lying unconscious on a cot.

"Felix!" Troy shook him.

Chad fought a surge of jealousy.

It's okay. Troy's fired up because Felix is Jesse's brother, Chad assured himself, and Jesse had been Troy's best friend. *And more*, Chad couldn't help but note.

Troy looked about frantically.

"He's drugged," Mandy said, kneeling next to Troy. "I'm sure he'll be fine once it wears off."

Troy nodded, squeezing Felix's hand.

"I'm here," Troy said to him. "I've got you."

Felix groaned, his eyes fluttered, and he looked at Troy drowsily.

"My Queero," Felix murmured before falling back asleep.

Chapter 9

The sound of birds chirping woke Raven. She'd had the strangest dream—about super-powered teens attacking. No matter what she did, she wasn't good enough, fast enough, or strong enough to stop them. How was she supposed to compete in a world like that?

The more she yielded to consciousness, the more her body ached. Seeped in pain, her eyes snapped open, and she popped up in bed.

She took in the scene—the Hummer in the middle of the bedroom, Pixie's smashed desk, and the steel door marked *WEAPON XY.* Raven sighed in relief. It was safely sealed shut. Those brats hadn't seen it or didn't know what to make of it. Either way, they left it alone.

Pixie sat next to her on the bed, sipping tea in a pair of overalls and a white tank top. Raven was no longer allowed to call such shirts wife-beaters.

"Good afternoon," Pixie said.

Raven took the ibuprofen Pixie offered, tossed them to the back of her throat, and dry swallowed.

"Status report?" Raven asked.

"Well, your Hummer's in our bedroom," Pixie began.

"I'm aware of that. The juicers—where are they?" Raven snapped.

"Gone," Pixie said.

Raven cupped her face.

"They left this," Pixie said, handing Raven a piece of glossy paper, torn from Troy's Paris Hilton journal. There was a photograph of the heiress in a yellow summer dress, arms raised in the air as if she were on a float and waving to fans. It was Paris' *Things I want everyone to know* page.

Handwriting was scrawled on it.

You know who we are; you know what we can do. Come for us again, and we'll be coming for you.

Raven rolled her eyes and crumpled the note. She winced as she got out of bed. The floor was swept of broken glass. Pixie had been busy. Raven pulled on a pair of cut-off jeans.

"All right, let's clean up your mess," Raven said, donning a pair of shades.

"*My* mess?" Pixie asked.

"I meant our mess," Raven backtracked. "I'm still woozy."

"My mess," Pixie repeated. "That's how you see this, isn't it? May I remind you that taking them by force was your idea?"

"You think your plan would've worked better?" Raven replied. She walked to the Hummer, popped open the rear, and pulled out a thick chain. It clattered to the floor.

"Well, maybe we give up then. Let Weapon XY walk free and call it a day," Pixie said, helping Raven hitch the chain to the back of the Hummer.

"That's not something you get to joke about," Raven replied, finger in the air, "not after what he did to us."

Pixie's lips pursed as Raven fed the chain out the hole in the wall.

Tears brimmed in Pixie's eyes. Raven let go of the chain, which clattered noisily to the ground.

"What did I say this time?" Raven asked.

"After what he did to us? *Us*?! Really, Raven?"

"All I meant was—"

"What Raven? What did you mean? That Weapon XY got *you* to lower *your* guard? That he fooled *you* into thinking that *you* were with the one *you* loved?"

"Pixie, I—

"Don't Raven. Don't even."

"I just meant—"

"I know what you meant," Pixie answered. "That somehow you were violated because he used his power to—"

"We need the crane to pull this out," Raven said, interrupting Pixie before she could finish the thought. Raven stared through the gaping hole in the side of the farmhouse, out at the field, towards the barn, anywhere but at Pixie.

"I sometimes think you blame me," Pixie said, "for not knowing it wasn't you, for not being able to tell the difference between an impostor and the woman I love. A part of you thinks I cheated on you."

Raven didn't know if it was because she was covered in stitches or a bunch of kids—*Chad*—had humiliated her, but she had no comforting lies to tell her girlfriend—only cold truth.

"I'd have known," Raven said. "It wouldn't have mattered how real the illusion. If positions were reversed, if he'd come to me disguised as you, I'd have seen through his mirage."

"I know you would have," Pixie whispered, staring at the steel door separating them from Weapon XY. It was a foot thick; to Raven, it always seemed paper-thin.

"I'm not you," Pixie added, standing next to Raven. She stared at the hole in the wall. It was going to be hell pulling the Hummer out and lowering it to the ground. Pixie wormed her way under Raven's arm. She softened enough to let Pixie snuggle.

Pixie spoke into her girlfriend's chest, "And that's why we're going to make sure no one, not him, not one of those juiced-up teenagers, not any of those other super-powered queers who are out there, no one will do what he did again."

"Capturing them didn't work," Raven said, hating to admit her failure, but there it was. "And I don't have the stomach to kill them."

"I want to show you something," Pixie said. She took her phone from a pocket in her overalls and placed it on the hood of the Hummer. At the swipe of the screen, a hologram projected directly above it, displaying two lines, jumping up and down. These were the brain scans Pixie tried to show her earlier. One belonged to "Romeo," the other to "Know-It-All."

"Do you see it?" Pixie asked.

Raven leaned in. "Right here," she said. "But that's not possible."

"It's not a glitch," Pixie assured her. "When Romeo was freaking out in the ambulance, his and Know-It-All's brainwaves were *identical*."

"But everybody's brainwaves are as unique as fingerprints," Raven said.

Pixie nodded fervently. "Somehow, unconscious, they were linked."

Raven smiled. "Does this mean—"

"We've found what we were praying for," Pixie interjected. "Goddess be praised."

"Goddess be praised," Raven echoed, though she didn't give a flying fart about the goddess. Still, her heart pounded with excitement, and her mind swirled with the possibilities.

"If all goes well, we won't need to lock those children in a cage," Pixie said. "Not once we put them on a leash."

Chapter 10

A few days later, Raven stared at the double doors that promised to change everything. They were painted red, with rectangular windows filled with security mesh. She cracked her neck and adjusted her blouse and suit jacket, dressed for the battle of her life. Her temples throbbed at the thought of those self-styled Queeroes. They believed they'd won, relishing the illusion that they could intimidate her with their freakish powers. Her fists clenched as she imagined them gathered around a cafeteria table, laughing at her.

"You're going down," she whispered. Pressing Chad's face into the floor with her heel was going to feel especially satisfying.

She released a deep breath and yanked the portal open. Her tours of duty in Iraq and Afghanistan meant nothing here. In the place of camouflaged fatigues, her slacks swished, and her heels clicked as she entered the greatest arena of all; the battlefield of all battlefields.

Raven was back in high school.

The squeal of hormonal teens falling in and out of love assaulted her ears, and the musky stench of sweat glands locked in overdrive violated her nose. Pubescent monsters packed the halls, fighting to get to classes they had little interest in attending. Raven assumed a margin of respect was her due, as a human being *and* an adult.

She hugged her gym bag to her chest, trying to push through the mob. "Excuse me," she said to no avail, banged one way and the other by a bevy of acne-prone punks.

One fool in a letterman jacket rammed her with his shoulder. He was a beefcake pretty boy. The name stitched into the arm of his jacket was *O'Reilly*. He reminded her of Troy and Jake.

"That's it!" she shouted.

She dropped her gym bag, wrenched Markham's arm behind his back, and pinned his cheek against a row of lockers.

"You will respect me, or, so help me, I'll shove your balls so far up your ass you'll be choking on them." The hallway fell dead silent. Not a single footstep or gossiped word was to be heard. She turned her head and felt like a rancher cornered by her cattle as the herd of students stared at her.

"For eff's sake," she swore. The little bastards were recording her on their cell phones.

She didn't know what was worse, the online attention this could draw or the lawsuit. In more civilized times, brats like this would get the strapping they deserved. Nowadays, teachers walked a minefield of political correctness that encouraged degeneracy. Raven wanted to discipline the kid all the more.

The mission, Raven, she reminded herself. She touched the metallic black stone in her jacket pocket. *Focus on the mission.*

Behind the students, Raven spied her salvation—a woman in drab janitorial gear who looked like she belonged in a boxing ring. *Chantal.* She held up a smartphone in a steampunk case with gears and anachronistic cogs on the back. Chantal clicked an App Pixie had designed, and a flash pulsed outwards; every device within twenty-five meters winked out. When they recharged, their owners would find they'd all reverted to factory settings and all data on them had been lost.

Raven mouthed an uncharacteristic *thank you* and dropped Markham.

"I am going to sue your ass," he threatened, readjusting his jacket.

Raven rounded on him. "You'll do nothing."

"You don't know who you're messing with," Markham snapped.

But she did. She recognized him now from their recon on the juicers. She leaned into him and whispered, "If you say a word, I'll tell Gibbie."

He stiffened, and his face went ashen. Gibbie was her enemy, but Markham didn't know that.

"If anyone asks, I was giving you self-defense lessons," she said.

The crowd parted for her as she strode confidently forward. Maybe high school wasn't so bad after all.

By the time she reached the gymnasium, Raven had abandoned the delusional thinking that a power suit would inspire deference. *It has shoulder pads!* she raged. *The most authoritative of all accessories!* She ducked into the women's washroom and corrected her mistake, changing into a no-nonsense navy blue tracksuit with red and white stripes down the arms and legs.

She emerged from the locker room and into the gym, her runners squeaking as she strode to center court. A few students watched her quizzically. None of them were on her list. The bell rang, and a throng of teens emerged from the change rooms, including three of her targets.

Mandy came from the left, leading a gaggle of girls. To the right were Chad and Troy, fingers entwined. Acid swirled in Raven's stomach. She couldn't hold her adult girlfriend's hand in public without being harassed in this piss-ass town, yet these two could go marching around in high school PDA-ing without a second thought? In the rest of the world, queers fought for that kind of change. These two took it for themselves, and only themselves, like the rest of their self-entitled generation.

It was Chad who noticed her first. He sniffed Raven's scent, making his eyes swivel in her direction. His jaw dropped. Raven smiled crookedly.

"Mister sisters," she mocked.

"What the hell are you doing here?" Chad snapped.

"She's the new women's gym teacher and cheerleading coach," Coach García's deep voice said from behind them. He shifted his beefy shoulders, stretching his white polo shirt this way and that. He was a hulk of a man and could've passed for an aging porn star. Raven admired his ability to keep it tight.

"Father," Chad enunciated with grand formality—and a curtsy.

"That's Coach García," Chad's dad informed him.

Chad rolled his eyes, "Yes, Coach."

Raven smirked. This was going to be fun. Troy seemed to agree. His twinkling eyes darted from Raven to Coach García's mustached face then back, drawing Raven's attention to the gooey-eyed look the coach was giving her.

She grabbed Troy by the arm, forcing him out of Coach García's hearing.

"I'm warning you, do not fool with me, boy," she said. "Whatever you're doing to Latinx Tom of Finland back there, you stop it right now. You do *not* have the right to mess with peoples' emotions."

Troy raised his hands innocently. "Nothing to do with me...*ma'am*."

"Hey!" Coach shouted at him. "Respect!"

Troy's attitude evaporated. "Yes, sir, sorry, sir," came from his Ken doll lips. He meant it, like a good indoctrinated soldier.

Interesting, Raven noted.

"To *her*," Coach jerked his head to Raven.

Though it looked like he was passing a gallstone, Troy managed an almost genuine, "Sorry."

To her surprise, Raven didn't hate it when the coach winked at her.

NOT THE WORST HAVING SOMEONE STICK UP FOR YOU, RIGHT?

The voice spoke in her head, but it didn't belong to her. She whipped around and stared into the face of one of her former prisoners, now reclassified in Pixie's dossier as an escapee. Raven touched the outline of the metallic stone in her pocket.

Control your thoughts, she ordered herself.

Felix's pretty mouth widened into a smile as his powerful arms tossed a basketball at her head.

THINK FAST.

She caught it half-an-inch from her face.

"Nice reflexes," Coach García approved.

"OMSF," Mandy commented, leaning her elbow on Chad's shoulder as Raven glared.

"Open Mouthed Shocked Face," Chad translated.

Raven forced her jaw closed.

They knew we'd be here, she thought.

YEAHS, WE DID. I'M A TELEPATH, REMEMBER? DID YOU THINK I WOULDN'T CHECK IN ON YOU? Felix asked in her mind.

"So, what, you and the rest of your frat brothers have gotten jobs here?" Raven asked Felix.

Mandy smirked, "Welcome to Nuffim High."

By midday, Raven considered it a miracle that she made it to the head guidance counselor's office without punching her fist through a wall. She yanked the door open and glared at Pixie seated behind a battered metal desk. The nameplate of her predecessor—one Gale Pedolwski—poked out of the trash. Gale suddenly quit to go on an all-expenses-paid world tour.

"Raven, I'm with a student," Pixie gestured at a teen girl sitting in a patched chair.

"Nobody likes me!" the student sobbed.

"Get out!" Raven shouted at her.

The girl froze.

"Now!"

Like a terrified gazelle, the girl grabbed her bag and rushed out the door.

"Dropping out *is* an option!" Raven yelled after her.

"It gets better!" Pixie shouted to the fleeing girl. To Raven, she said, "Is this the kind of teacher you're going to be? What happened to the idealist I fell in love with?"

"I'm a realist idealist. Bomb the enemy. *That's* democracy."

"Rough day?" Pixie asked.

"I don't know who's worse, the kids or the teachers," Raven agreed. "Some hunchbacked octogenarian lectured me in the teacher's lounge about washing my coffee cup."

"You do have a habit of leaving it in the sink," Pixie admonished.

"Take his side, why don't you?" Raven pouted. "Oh, and the telepath is here," she added as an afterthought.

"Yes," Pixie said, "I'd noticed that. Muriel, show us target Know-It-All."

"*Right away, ma'am,*" Muriel flirted.

Pixie's e-pad projected a hologram upwards. Raven watched Felix walking with Mandy, Chad, and Troy.

"What about the others?" Raven asked.

"Muriel…"

Before Pixie could finish the sentence, Muriel switched the scene, showing Blake sitting with Gibbie in a home-ec class. Gibbie struggled with the piping on a triple layer cake. Unasked, Muriel shifted the hologram to show a miserable Alejandro wearing janitor's overalls, pinching his nose as he dusted sawdust onto a circle of puke.

"They still use that stuff?" Raven asked in awe. "What about Trick?"

"*The teleporter?*" Muriel asked. "*Negative.*"

Pixie shrugged. "We've wired the whole school, but no sign of him." She flipped through several more scenes, making the e-pad giggle.

"*That tickles,*" Muriel said, showing the biology lab, the gym, English classes, math classes, a hallway, another hallway, and the weight room where several muscled jocks pumped iron and vied for space in front of a floor-to-ceiling mirror.

"Nada," said Pixie.

"At least the rest of them fell for it," Raven smiled.

"Yes," Pixie agreed, tapping the black stone about her throat. "We let them glean just enough from our minds to be exactly where we wanted them to be."

"I'm not sure we can pull this off," Raven said. The words grated her throat.

Pixie smiled, flirtatiously plopping herself in the muscular woman's lap.

"Conning them all into one place was the hard part," Pixie kissed Raven lightly. "Winning them over will be easy. You'll see."

Chapter 11

"So you absorb energy," Gibbie said to Blake. "That's so cool."

Gibbie was decorating a vanilla cake in home economics. He picked up a blue space invader made from sugar and food coloring and placed it into gooey icing.

"Except for this," Blake said, grabbing his flab. "I used to be skinnier than you. All I wanted was to bulk up. I guess I should've been more specific."

"You are who you are. Own it," Gibbie said.

"Maybe," Blake said uncertainly. "I still think you're lucky to be so cute."

Gibbie didn't register that Blake had called him cute. It was hard to focus on anything with brawny Desirée at the front of the class; she'd replaced the grandma-esque Mrs. McReally after a lawyer pointed out an unnoticed clause in her contract allowing for an oddly generous early retirement package.

"Are we supposed to pretend it's normal that the unhinged women who kidnapped you and your friends are now working at our school?" Gibbie asked.

"Don't worry, Felix will think of something," Blake assured him.

"I dunno; my brother Troy's pretty good at coming up with plans. Might beat him to it," Gibbie said earnestly.

"I bet you come up with good plans," Blake offered shyly, sticking his finger into the icing bowl and licking it clean.

"I'm more the research guy," Gibbie said. "I've got a whole presentation ready. You're coming, right?"

"Yes!" Blake said then tried to conceal his enthusiasm. "I mean, yeah, sure, united we stand and all that."

"Exactly," Gibbie said. "We can't let them divide us."

"Don't worry; I've got every single class with you," Blake said.

"What?" Gibbie asked, turning the cake around so he could unleash more alien attackers on its sugary surface. "Why?"

"So we can watch out for each other," Blake said.

Gibbie considered this, squeezing a piping bag. "How do you know my class schedule?"

Blake looked to the side. "I may have hacked the school computer system."

"Nice," Gibbie conceded.

"Yeah," Blake agreed, "and since I skipped a few grades, I never took home economics. This is fun!"

Markham walked by and tripped over Blake's bag. "Watch where you put that thing, lard ass!" Markham snapped. He looked ready to start something until Gibbie stood up.

"Oh, sorry, didn't see you, Gibbie," Markham blushed.

Desirée coughed loudly at Gibbie. He glared but sat down.

"I hate it when that guy gets away with stuff," Gibbie huffed.

"Want to try something cool?" Blake asked, looking at Markham as he cracked an egg into a bowl.

"Does it involve teaching Markham a lesson?" Gibbie asked.

"Maybe," Blake blinked.

"I'm in," Gibbie grinned.

"Press your palm to mine," Blake said, holding up his hand.

Gibbie mirrored his new friend. Their skin met. A gentle warmth spread from Blake to Gibbie.

"Are you discharging energy?" Gibbie asked.

Blake's hand glowed red, and tendrils of crimson energy flowed from him into the small boy. Gibbie smiled with pleasure.

"That feels amazing," Gibbie said.

"Now clap your hands together," Blake said. Gibbie was about to do so when Blake stopped him. "Not towards the cake!" he said. He angled Gibbie to face Markham who whisked his eggs with surprisingly sure strokes.

"What's the macronutrient breakdown of this recipe?" Markham asked.

Gibbie clapped, and the force sent a ripple of air pounding into his nemesis. Markham flew off his seat, followed by his bowl and unused eggs, which smashed into him an instant later. He picked a shell off his dripping chest and stared at it in disbelief.

The class of teens gaped. Blake and Gibbie struggled to contain their laughter. Their "teacher" glared.

"How did I do that?" Gibbie asked.

"I supercharged your super strength," Blake explained. "I've done it to Alejandro when he's a bigger D than usual. Made him phase right through the floor."

"I wonder what else we could do," Gibbie mused, making Blake's eyes light up.

"This is cool," he beamed. "If not for those women, we might never have met. Some particle physicists think that nothing's chance—that every action is the predictable reaction to the big bang still playing out."

"All the world's a particle accelerator—" Gibbie began.

"And we are just Boson particles upon it," Blake finished for him.

They laughed, setting down their icing dispensers to gaze at their cake. It lilted to one side.

"It's kind of ugly," Gibbie admitted.

"I bet it's delicious," Blake replied, staring at Gibbie. The little guy was focused on the cake.

"Listen," Blake said, "not to go all Canadian pop sensation on you, but… I know we just met, and this *is* crazy, but—"

His words were cut short by a swirling cyclone of purple-pink energy. They were seated in the back corner of the classroom, so no one else noticed—except for their teacher. She sat up, dropped her magazine of *Folk Music Weekly*, and fired off a text. The lavender light was gone in a hot second, and across from Gibbie and Blake sat a muscular youth in a ribbed tank top.

Gibbie's eyes widened.

"Jake!"

Blake noted the worship electrifying Gibbie's voice and demeanor. Light glinted off the faux diamonds in Jake's ears.

"Hey, Jake," Blake said unenthusiastically. "We were wondering when you'd show. Had to be now, I guess."

Jake looked around. "Home ec?" he asked.

"What gave it away?" Blake asked.

"Chad and I used to sneak in here to…play house." His attention veered to the cake on the table in front of them. He eyed the glucose-filled space invaders ravenously. "Do you mind if I—"

"We're saving it for later," Blake interrupted. "Gibbie's got an amazing presentation for us, and we thought the whole group might enjoy—"

Jake wasn't listening. He was glassy-eyed as he grabbed a fork, stabbed it into the dessert, and shoved a bite into his mouth.

"Or you could have some now," Blake conceded, sitting on his stool with a thud.

"Oh my God," Jake said between bites.

"Is it good?" Gibbie asked, eyes begging for Jake's approval.

"You have no idea. I have got to start packing more power bars to get me through these teleports."

After mowing down on half the cake, Jake's eating slowed, and his breathing grew even. He noticed Blake's look of disdain. Jake pulled his fork from his mouth and stared at the ravaged dessert, realizing what he'd done.

"Guys, I'm so sorry. I will so buy you a new cake. I've been trying to teleport back since yesterday and kept bouncing all over. I've barely eaten. I think one more trip would've killed me."

"I guess that means we saved your life," Gibbie said.

"I guess so," Jake smiled, rustling Gibbie's hair. "I am in your debt."

Desirée slammed her ruler on the desk. All eyes turned front.

"No talking," she ordered.

Jake gawked.

"What's *she* doing here?"

"Oh my Jean-Luc Picard," Gibbie replied, helping himself to a plastic forkful of cake, "have I got a presentation for you."

Chapter 12

YOU OKAY? Felix asked Troy telepathically. They sat in a darkened classroom with the rest of the Queeroes. Gibbie stood at the front, backlit by the glare of a projector hooked up to his laptop. A clip from an animated superhero series ran behind him.

"...so as we can see, the importance of teamwork cannot be overestimated," Gibbie explained.

A little weirded out, Troy confessed. He shifted in his seat as if he could make room in his mind for Felix's presence by moving over a couple of inches. *Part of me feels like I cheated on Chad.*

SAME! Felix agreed. *I KEEP WANTING TO TELL ALEJANDRO WHAT HAPPENED, BUT NOTHING HAPPENED; IT WAS A DREAM.*

Exactly! Troy "said," though not a word was spoken aloud. *Weird stuff happens in dreams all the time. It doesn't count once you wake up.*

RIGHT!

"...here's another perfect example," Gibbie continued, the image shifting to a scene from a blockbuster sequel. "Here we see a group of outcasts not only working together, but also teaming up with their arch nemesis..."

Troy's eyes shifted to Felix. It was nice having his voice in his head.

IT'S NICE HAVING YOUR VOICE IN MY HEAD, TOO, Felix replied to the unspoken thought.

"What's so funny?" Chad whispered from the desk next to Troy's. Jake kept eyeing Chad.

"What?" Troy said, realizing he was smiling goofily from Felix's presence in his mind. Troy stifled a laugh from Felix playfully singing 'Girls Just Want To Have Fun' in Troy's head, too distracted to notice the lust pouring off Jake every time he glanced at Chad.

"Brain fart," Troy explained.

"Shhh," Mandy glared, giving them dagger eyes. *Stupid couples.*

I CAN HEAR YOU, Felix told her.

Can you see images too, or just hear people's inner monologues? Mandy asked.

BOTH.

She formed a picture of herself lifting her middle finger.

"...and so," Gibbie concluded in the glare of the projector's light as the montage of images behind him ended on a Hollywood hunk in tights with a super-powered ring in a celluloid flop, "that is our best course of action."

Gibbie stared at his assembled Queeroes—his brother Troy, friends Mandy and Chad, and *new* friends Alejandro, Felix, Blake, and (swoon) Jake. Gibbie awaited their applause.

He was rewarded by the lonesome patter of Blake's palms slapping together. When no one else joined in, he blushed, and his applause petered out.

"That was retarded," Alejandro broke the ensuing silence. "Sorry, mentally delayed." His jet black hair was swooped back, and he'd tied a red bandana around his neck as if that could jazz up his janitor's uniform.

"Alejandro—" Felix began.

"Stop," Alejandro snapped. "Why are we listening to pale Urkel?"

"That's my brother you're talking about," Troy said with a dangerous edge.

"Your nerd-tarded brother wasted forty-five minutes of my life, which I will never get back, to give us a presentation on the importance of teamwork, basing his argument on the oh so credible scenarios depicted in comic book spin-offs, including," Alejandro pointed to the screen, "one of the worst movies ever made."

"It was not a triumph," Gibbie conceded. He was surprised that anyone here (other than Blake) had seen Tinsel Town's failed attempt to turn an intergalactic cadre wielding the power of green light into a franchise. Gibbie had chosen it for its hunky blond star, figuring that would hold this lot's attention better than an old wizard waving a wooden staff and shouting, "You shall not pass!"

"To be fair," Blake said, adjusting his T-shirt, "Gibbie restricted himself to material the rest of you could identify with—too soon reboots produced by four-quadrant obsessed studios that pump out unnecessarily altered characters and special-effects-driven plotlines for the bleating masses."

"Superheroes aren't just for geeks anymore," Mandy countered. "They've gone mainstream."

"You're a bimbo," Alejandro replied.

"You have puke on your shoes," Mandy said.

There were muffled laughs from Chad, Troy, and Blake. Felix struggled to control his face. Alejandro looked at them darkly.

"Guys," Gibbie squeaked, hating that his voice still did that, "this is what they want—for us to turn on each other."

"I've seen enough," Alejandro said to Gibbie, then to Felix, "Babe, let's get out of here."

He took Felix's hand and began phasing them through the floor into the classroom below. They got ankle deep when a knock at that door made them pause. It opened, revealing Pixie and Raven.

"Sorry to interrupt, but we have this room reserved for five minutes ago," Pixie said with pained regret. She was dressed like a Catholic private-school girl, wearing a plaid pleated skirt, stark dress jacket, and a red skinny-tie. Raven towered over her in a blue tracksuit accented with racing stripes.

The Queeroes stared, muscles tensed. Gibbie attempted to shut down his computer before they could see his top-secret presentation, which resulted in his finger smashing through his keyboard and breaking the desk beneath into two.

"Not again!" he whined.

Raven closed the door.

"Full disclosure," Pixie continued, "we've got the whole school wired, sound *and* video. You can stop trying to hide your presentation Gibbie. We saw it the ten times you rehearsed it earlier. And you two," she said to Alejandro and Felix, "you might as well come up out of the floor. You look ridiculous."

They floated into the classroom.

"Better," Pixie nodded. "Anywho, your whole teamwork thesis sounds great. Thumbs up. Just want to make one thing super-duper clear before you go full throttle with that. We're not your enemies."

"You kidnapped us," Alejandro said, trying to cut her with his gaze.

"Eye-roll," Pixie replied, giving Chad a wink.

"That's my line," Chad said. "Stealing catchphrases is *not* okay."

"What about the part where they Big Brothered us?" Jake said.

"Yeah," Gibbie agreed, trying to squeeze the broken pieces of his computer back together.

"Morally questionable, I agree," Pixie said. "But, for a generation addicted to posting your every burp on social media, I have a news flash. You are not that interesting."

"Then, why are you here?" Troy challenged.

"Sweetie," Pixie said as if she were a shoe-addicted sex columnist trying to find love in the Big Apple, "the answer is obvious. We're here to help."

She smiled at their blank stares, pulled out her phone, and held it towards the screen.

"Muriel," was all Pixie had to say and the image of a hunky hero fizzled away, replaced by a trio of photos that silenced the group immediately.

"Your classmates," Pixie said, her voice quiet and serious. "*Former* classmates."

It was Liza, Devon, and Jesse. Curvaceous Liza smiled in her picture, making the peace sign with her fingers. Devon was next to her, in full Goth mode, staring sullenly. Jesse's arms bulged as he gripped a football on the field, ready to make a pass. Pixie looked to Troy, Jesse's best friend, and Felix, Jesse's brother. Their jaws clenched, daring her to say the wrong thing.

"Being a teenager is tough enough without the added factor of your unique abilities," Pixie said. She pointed to the screen. "We've seen what can happen when teenage life and superpowers collide. Last time, three young people lost their lives."

"We're not like them," Mandy said.

"Is that so?" Pixie pressed another button. Video played of Blake supercharging Gibbie, and Gibbie sending Markham flying from his seat with a clap. Another video took over, of Chad doing an impossible series of flips at a cheerleading competition—then being handed a giant trophy.

"Would you believe it was the catnip?" he asked.

"Moving on," Pixie said. A new video popped up, showing Mandy walking into Aberbombie and Stitch, picking up a shirt, and popping off the security tag with her forcefield. Everyone watched her turn invisible, only to be caught by Chad as she was sneaking out.

Mandy scoffed. "I was tired of Chad neglecting me."

"Shoplifting to get attention?" Pixie asked. "This is the stable mental character of the individual who can pass unseen whenever she chooses?"

Mandy opened her mouth to protest.

"Don't," Pixie advised her.

"It was just a shirt," Chad said, staring at Raven challengingly.

"Was Jesse just a shirt when Mandy chose to take a video of him and Troy making out? The video that contributed to his suicide?" Pixie asked pointedly. Before Troy or Felix could say anything, she added, "Was Jesse just a shirt when Chad told Mandy to go into that change room, catching Troy and Jesse together? Were you just shirts when Devon and Liza turned you against each other, almost killing one another?"

Pixie gazed at them. "You're a time bomb of hormones and social pressure. You're out of control. All of you."

"I repeat, you kidnapped us," Alejandro said, pointing to himself, Felix, and Blake. "Who does that?"

"We know about the robbery," Pixie replied. "How you walked through walls and stole from your father's safety deposit box."

"He cut me off when he found out I was gay," Alejandro snapped back. "You sure you want to take his side?"

"Gibbie," Pixie said, "what does that make Alejandro? Does that make him a hero? Does it make him a Queero?"

"No," Gibbie said, the answer causing him pain.

"What does it make him?" Pixie pressed.

Gibbie looked around sheepishly, an expert defense witness forced to take the side of the prosecution. "It makes him a villain." Like tectonic plates settling into place after a quake, he sighed, "We've all been acting like villains."

"And there's this," Pixie said, tossing a battered plaque onto a desk. Jake recognized it from the gayternity. It read, *Enter to serve, go forth to rule.*

"Sounds very world domination to me," Pixie accused. "When you're ready, come talk to me, as a group or one-by-one. I'm the new school counselor. I'm here to help. We all are. To help you grow into the fine young adults we know you can be. If you truly want to be Queeroes, you need guidance."

"Muriel," Pixie said, and an iconic bald man in a wheelchair appeared on the display screen. Pixie smiled.

"Think of me as your Professor XX."

Chapter 13

A few hours later, Raven sat in Pixie's school counselor's office, leaning back in a chair, her sneakered feet up on the desk. "Do you think they bought it?" Raven tossed a tennis ball at the wall, caught it, then tossed it again.

"They will." Pixie shuffled through holographic charts, readings, and graphs, making Muriel giggle as if being tickled.

"Pretty bold of you, telling them the truth like that," Raven said. "It was kind of hot."

Pixie nodded distractedly. "Come on, where are you..."

Raven waited futilely for her flirtation to filter through Pixie's distraction. Instead…

"*I'm sorry my search algorithm crashed after Raven spilled her energy drink on me*," Muriel apologized in an accusing tone.

Raven caught the tennis ball, squeezed it with irritation, then pitched it through the holographic data, making it swirl.

Pixie turned to her. "I find you sexually desirable as well, and when I find what I'm looking for, I will reward myself with physical gratification. Until then..." Pixie turned back to her data.

"Muriel, mute," Raven said before the AI could gloat, "or I'll smash your speakers." The program grumbled then went silent.

Raven came to Pixie's side.

"We've got this whole school wired," Pixie said. "Those kids haven't popped a zit without Muriel encoding it." Pixie pulled up several holographic screens, playing images of the Queeroes. "What am I missing?"

"Let's sleep on it," Raven said. "Everything will be clearer in the morning."

"Sleep on it," Pixie murmured. She eyed her girlfriend up and down. "Could it be that simple?"

"No," Raven said. "Whatever you're thinking, I'm not doing it. *Please* stop looking at me like that!"

"Sorry, babe," Pixie replied, pulling up a video of Chad talking with his dad. It was time-stamped from an hour ago. Chad gesticulated dramatically; his father barely noticed. The video showed Coach García staring at Raven, who was bossing around Mandy and the rest of the cheerleading squad.

Turning a holographic dial, Pixie increased the volume.

"García!" holo Raven shouted in crackly audio from the e-pad speaker. "Get those short shorts back here!"

Chad scurried away from his dad, who shook his head at his son's rear determined to fall out of his customized cheerleader's uniform.

"What?" holographic Raven demanded of the coach as the events of a few hours ago replayed.

"You shouted García," Coach said. "I thought you were talking to me."

"I wasn't." Holo Raven turned to her squad, screaming into her megaphone, "This is a bigger car wreck than the final scene of *Thelma and Louise*!"

Holo Coach's male gaze was unrelenting. "We should grab a beer sometime," he said. Holo Raven replied, "We really shouldn't." In real time, Pixie raised a brow. Raven's cheeks burned, and her eyes dropped.

"When were you going to mention the head coach has the hots for you?" Pixie asked.

"What?" Raven said. "Shut it. Not only is he a dick, he *has* a dick."

"Relationships work on trust," Pixie admonished, arms folded over her petite chest. Rainbow light flashed briefly from the metallic stone about her neck. "We can't be going around with secrets. It's toxic."

"That isn't funny," Raven said.

"This is," Pixie winked, picking up an old-fashioned microphone. Pixie pressed one of the worn buttons on its base and announced, "Coach García to the school counselor's office. That's Coach García to the school counselor's office." Her message gargled over the school's antiquated PA system.

"What are you doing?" Raven demanded.

"We need data," Pixie said. "That means *you* are going on a date."

As Coach García was drawn unawares into Pixie's scheme, across town, in the basement of the Allstar residence, four Queeroes converged.

Troy watched himself in a mirror, finishing up a set of standing biceps curls, his arms bulging melons in his yellow Aberbombie tank.

"How weird is it that Jake Kanaan is back?" Troy said, switching to triceps extensions. "And he can teleport. Who would've guessed he was gay?"

Chad and Mandy looked at each other in the midst of their handstand push-ups. Gibbie was engrossed in a video game, his free hand easily pressing a stack of forty-five-pound plates. Chad landed nimbly on his feet.

"I mean, the guy was the straightest," Troy observed, setting the weight down and flexing his guns.

"Uhm, about that," Chad began, looking to Mandy for support. She lowered her legs and picked up a skipping rope.

"This is going to be reality TV at its best," she said.

Troy paused his second set of biceps curls and stared at his boyfriend. "Why are you feeling guilty?"

"Guilty?" Chad scoffed. "You're on crack."

"Is he?" Mandy asked, her jump rope whooshing.

"Goddamn it!" Gibbie cursed. His phone blipped and bleeped. "Blake's paratroopers have my cyborg army surrounded. Unless..." He pushed his thumb onto the screen of his phone; it snapped in half—like his computer earlier. His mouth dropped, his eyes widened, and his other hand went limp—the stack of plates he'd been hefting clattered to the floor.

"First, my computer; now this?!" Gibbie cursed to the uncaring heavens. "I was going to use my electro blast to decommission Blake's army!"

Troy smirked, racked his weights, and ruffled his brother's hair. "Relax, Gibster. I'll encourage the gay at the Einstein Bar to replace it for free—again."

Chad was relieved that Troy had been distracted. Chad was equally pissed that his boyfriend was that quick to forget about him. Troy resumed his biceps curls, arms puffing with each rise of the weight. Chad intensified his displeasure. Troy was oblivious. Tonight was a Gibbie episode. The kid grew more forlorn, trying to press the two pieces of his phone back together.

"What's the matter?" Troy asked, hissing as he eked out more reps.

"Using your powers to get a free phone is the kind of thing a villain would do," Gibbie said.

"Don't let Pixie and her maniacs get to you," Mandy said. "The manufacturer can afford it."

"That's what a villain would say," Gibbie replied.

"Come on," Troy added, "I'm your big bro. I'm going to look out for you."

"Maybe," Gibbie said doubtfully. "It's just, sometimes we're more like the Masters of Mayhem than the Hall of Heroics."

"Isn't Court of Queeroes more on brand?" Troy quipped.

Normally, Chad would applaud his boyfriend's bold incursion into the realm of wordplay, but not if it meant being overlooked.

"Gibbie," Mandy added, "you don't think we should do what those devils who don't wear Prada say?"

"No!" Gibbie said. "Yes? I don't know. I like not being bullied. I like sticking up for my friends. But, part of me *enjoys* pushing Markham around."

"Tell you what; if you turn into a douche, we'll let you know. And vice versa, yeah?" Troy said. He looked to Chad and Mandy for support.

"Deal," Mandy agreed, turning to her bestie meaningfully. "So Chad…"

Chad remained silent. *Is Mandy right? Am I a douche for not telling Troy about Jake?* Chad tried upping his feeling of guilt to regain his boyfriend's attention, but Troy was focused on his brother.

"An anti-douche pact seems to lack the necessary gravitas for the current scenario," Gibbie said. "Pixie has a point. Jesse did kill himself, and—"

"Stop right there," Troy said. "She had no right bringing up Jesse, and in front of Felix? That's bull. Pure and simple."

The intensity of Troy's feelings smacked everyone in the room. Chad noted it peaked when Troy mentioned Felix.

"Sorry," Troy said, taking a deep breath and sending out soothing waves.

Chad let go a gentle breath, absorbing the warm balm. *Finally!*

"What *did* you sense from Pixie and Raven?" Gibbie asked.

"It was weird," Troy said, doing bench dips. "They're controlled. I only got flashes, and their feelings kept changing. I think they were doing it on purpose to throw me off. Felix couldn't read much from their minds either."

"When did you and Felix talk about that?" Chad asked in the midst of double-unders, the skipping rope singing in repetitive whooshes.

"It was real quick," Troy said in a rush. Chad caught the rise in his body odor, and an increase in the drip of his sweat. Chad's insecurity flared. *Maybe I'm not the one with something to hide.* Double-unders became triple-unders; the rope whooshed so fast, it snapped.

"The point is," Troy filled the ensuing silence, "we can't trust them. But we can trust each other. So that's what we do. We have each other's backs; we help each other stay in line; we make sure we all stay the good guys."

"Good *guys*? Watch the gendered nouns," Gibbie chided. "But, fine. I know when I'm outnumbered."

"And outgunned," Troy grinned, flexing his biceps.

Gibbie gave him sour-face. "Douche alert."

Chad worried Gibbie was more right than he knew.

Chapter 14

Meanwhile, one town over, in Hardman Hall, known to locals as the gayternity…

"This is bullcrap," Alejandro cursed. He wore bright yellow overalls, no shirt, his shoulder-length hair tied back with an orange bandana. He stood on a step ladder, applying plaster to their busted-up dining room.

"Aye carrumba," Blake agreed as he pressed away on his e-pad; blips and bleeps of video game machine gun fire rose from the speaker.

"That is not something Latinxs say," Alejandro said. "That's something white people say Latinxs say."

"I've got you now!" Blake tittered without looking up. "Yes, yes, yes!" His face beamed, followed by a perplexed furrow across his brow. "That's weird. It looked like Gibbie was about to unleash his electro-blast. That would've completely incapacitated my unit."

"He's not watching porn, is he," Alejandro said. It wasn't a question.

Felix shrugged, blue-bagging the last of the shot up Etienne water bottles. He wore a sleeveless shirt that flattered his arms. Bits of muscular leg peeked through his ripped track pants.

"For him, I think that is porn," Felix smiled.

"This is weird," Blake said, his phone to his ear. "Gibbie's not picking up."

"He's just not that into you," Alejandro explained, his words falling on deaf ears.

"I better go over there," Blake said. "Make sure he's okay, you know, with everything that's going on."

A smile played on Felix's lips. "In that case, maybe we should all go."

"Good idea," Blake replied, putting on his jacket. "You guys stay here and hold down the fort."

The door slammed shut behind him. Felix smirked while Alejandro made gagging noises.

"You're fooling no one. You love that he's in love," Felix teased.

"Gross," Alejandro replied.

"Is that why you thought 'you go girl' as he walked by?" Felix pressed.

"Do not read my mind," Alejandro said.

"No?"

"No."

Felix came closer, wrapping his arms around Alejandro and lifting him off the step ladder. "Not even a little?"

"Not even," Alejandro agreed.

"Not when you're thinking you want me to kiss you?"

Alejandro appeared aghast. "Especially then!"

He phased himself out Felix's arms and landed on the floor behind him.

"I may be evil, according to those women," Alejandro said, "but that don't mean I'm easy."

"You've always been challenged," Felix agreed.

"Is it my ESL, or was that an insult?" Alejandro countered.

Felix pressed his boyfriend against the wall. "You were born in Connecticut."

"I could phase right out of this," Alejandro said.

Felix kissed him passionately. "I love your lips. Do that thing that you do."

"Yeah?"

"Yeah."

They kissed longer and deeper. Alejandro used his power, phasing his tongue into Felix's tongue, his lips into Felix's lips. As they drew apart, Alejandro unphased lips and tongue both, not enough for them to get stuck together, but, for two heartbeats, neither could tell where one began and the other ended.

"I'm going to get the shower started," Alejandro said.

"You could phase free of the dirt," Felix replied.

"More fun if you help me," Alejandro winked, slipping away from his boyfriend. Manipulating his power, he floated up and disappeared through the ceiling.

"Yum," Felix said, rubbing his chest.

He grabbed the balustrade, ready to bound up the stairs when a loud knock came at the door.

He groaned. "Blake, I love you like a love song, but stop forgetting your keys!"

Felix yanked the portal open.

There stood Pixie.

Alone.

As Felix stared at enemy one-of-four, back in Nuffim, Troy, Chad, Gibbie, and Mandy wrapped up their calisthenics and weight training and said their goodbyes.

Outside the Allstar residence, Chad got on behind Troy on his motorbike. He ably navigated it along an empty road. Chad knew that with his powers, he could do flips and wheelies without breaking a sweat, but he loved having Troy at the controls.

Do you love it? Do you love being less than you could be so he feels like more in the relationship? the animal in Chad growled. *He completes me*, Chad thought back to his feral voice. *Let me be happy!* That other part of him hissed, *Then tell him about Jake.* Chad promised himself he would, *As soon as we get to my house.*

Troy turned into a subdivision and stopped in front of the García residence. Any thought of a heart-to-heart evaporated. They took off their helmets and stared at the black Mad Max Hummer sitting in the driveway.

"What the eff?" Troy swore, fingers forming a fist.

Chad's ears grew pointed; his teeth became fangs. A woman's laughter rose from an open window, followed by a man's shy, amused chortle.

"Oh, hell's no," Chad said, storming the door.

Earlier that day, Raven found herself doing the unthinkable—asking out a guy.

It started with Pixie calling for the coach on the school's loudspeaker. As soon as he arrived in the counselor's office, Pixie slipped past him. He watched her go, confused.

I'm going to kill her, Raven thought, her heart hammering madly.

Raven had not been on a proper date since high school.

Martha Chowder was the girl's name. She'd had big breasts, braces, and had been a powerhouse on the women's wrestling team. It was she who'd gone blabbing to the whole school after one make-out session with Raven, telling every mean girl in town, which was every girl in town as far as Raven was concerned, that Raven was a raging dyke—like everyone suspected.

Since then, she could rhyme off a short list of meaningless encounters that ended when she met Pixie.

The things I'll do for that woman, Raven thought, but going on a date with Coach García?

She didn't like this guy, didn't like men period. Yet, now that she had to ask him out, all she could think was, *I don't want him to say no*, though she didn't want him to say "yes," either.

He looked from Raven to where Pixie had disappeared then back to Raven. "Is Chad in trouble? He's a good kid. A little, you know..." he twirled his wrists. "Swishy?"

"Expressive," the coach said. "Not that there's anything wrong with that."

"You wish he were more butch," Raven said.

"Could you teach him?" Coach asked.

The hopefulness in his face and voice! She laughed, and when he looked confused, she laughed louder. He broke a shy smile.

He's more scared than I am, Raven realized; that softened her, a little. She despised weakness yet found it hard to shake the habit of defending the defenseless.

"Chad's fine," she reassured him.

"Good. What about you? Are you settling into the school okay?"

"It's very high-schoolish," she said.

"It being a high school."

Awkward silence.

"Do you wanna," he indicated vaguely towards the hall with his thumb.

"Oh, no," she replied, avoiding his gaze as she shuffled some papers around on Pixie's desk.

Damn it damn it damn it! Stop being such a spaz! This is why she'd tanked her Secret Service interview. Cool under military fire, shrapnel under social duress.

"Are you sure? Because I've been at this school a long time, and this feels like..." his words trailed off. "You know what, never mind. I guess your friend called me in here by mistake." He turned away, reaching for the door handle.

"Coach García!" Raven shouted. She meant to sound like a drill sergeant, not a teenage girl.

He turned hopefully.

"Yes," she said.

"Yes, what?" he asked.

"Yes to..." she pointed vaguely towards the hall. "Yes to that thing, you suggested earlier."

He looked puzzled.

"You know," she twirled her hand. "A date." The words were barbed wire coming up her throat, and they sent a rush of fire to her cheeks. To her disappointment—and relief—he said, "I'm in."

To Raven's surprise, their dinner together hadn't sucked. Finally, someone she could talk to about race cars, football, and firearms! Not once did he bring up cats, vegetarianism, or homemade reusable menstrual pads. They drank beer, not wine, ate wings instead of tofu, and both took their coffee black, balking in unison at the waiter's offer of herbal tea. There was even something sexy about his brawny arms and cartoonish mustache.

Getting him to invite her back to his place was too easy.

In his tidy, dated kitchen with a cross above the fridge, he popped open a pair of beers. As they clinked bottles, Raven saw Troy's motorcycle pull up front.

"Here's to drinking on a school night," she said, laughing intentionally loudly. He guffawed in return.

She spied Troy and Chad racing down the driveway. To bolster her courage, she took a long swig from the bottle; before she could chicken out, she leaned in for the kiss. Her lips met the coach's as the teens burst through the doorway.

Screw you CIA, she thought. *I* am *secret agent material.*

Coach García pulled back in surprise. Raven's smirk marred her performance, but the fury on Chad's face saved the show.

"What the hell are you doing here?" Chad demanded.

"Language," Coach said.

"You stay away from my dad," Chad warned.

Coach García sighed. "I'm sorry, Raven. I haven't dated anyone since his mother died. And you know how he can be a little..." Coach twirled his wrist.

"Expressive?" Raven smiled. They laughed as if at an inside joke.

Chad gaped, one fist planted on his hip, the pointy finger of his other hand raised in the air in his judgemental teapot pose. "This is not funny."

"You're right," Raven said. "Don't worry, Chad; you don't have to call me Mamá, yet."

She and Coach laughed again.

"You're drunk. You're both drunk," Chad said with disgust.

"I'm going to finish my beer then head home," Raven said. "No harm, no foul."

"Except that you're a lesb—" Chad started to shriek.

The crash of shattering glass cut him off. White fizz splattered across the floor. "Did I drop my beer," Raven said with mock astonishment. "How clumsy of me." She gave Chad a warning look.

"You're still a lesb—"

"Troy!" Raven interrupted. "Why don't you stay for the night?"

"What?" Troy asked.

"What?" Chad echoed.

"What?" Chad's dad chimed in.

"It's late to be riding around on that motorbike," Raven said.

"You should go," Coach said to Troy.

"You should stay," Raven countered.

"Raven, there's no overnighters here," Chad's dad said.

"None?" Raven said with disappointment, unzipping her track jacket to reveal a flash of cleavage in her lacy bra.

She reached to the fridge, her flat, muscular chest brushing against the coach's, and she helped herself to another beer. She winked at him as she popped the lid off with a bottle opener then slid her lips around the rim.

She felt a fool with this whole sex-kitten schtick.

What am I doing? she demanded of herself. *He's going to laugh me right out of here!*

"That's uh, quite the uh..." Coach García was at a loss for words.

Is he into this? Men! Yet, Raven felt a touch proud of herself.

"I'm going to get the broom to clean this up," he stammered.

"Off you go, boys," Raven said with growing confidence, shooing the teens with her hands. "Up to Chad's room with you."

They remained planted.

"You heard the lady!" Coach García shouted. "Move!"

Unsure what else to do, the teens shuffled towards the stairs.

"Don't try anything," Troy said to her as he passed. "I'm keeping tabs on you." He tapped his temple in warning.

"Understood," she said, knowing that in a few moments she'd be the last thing on his hormonal mind.

Back at the gayternity...

"Felix, what is taking you so long?" Alejandro demanded, poking his head down through the ceiling. His shirtless delts and upper pecs peeked through; he gaped at the sight of Pixie in the doorway. "What is *she* doing here?"

"I'm not sure," Felix admitted.

"You're a telepath," Alejandro said.

"She's difficult to read," Felix admitted.

"Frustrating, isn't it?" Pixie asked, toying with the metallic stone around her neck. Shifting in the light, it momentarily flashed a multitude of colors in the pattern of circuitry. "I'm here to return this," she said, handing over the beaten-up plaque that was once bolted above the doorway.

Felix took it, reading it. *Enter to serve, go forth to rule.* "We never meant anything by this," he said.

"We should talk," Pixie said.

Felix sighed. "Agreed."

Alejandro groaned, knowing what that meant for him. He rolled his eyes as he withdrew, muttering in his wake, "Lesbians are the worst."

At the García residence, Troy and Chad stood side by side, looking at his bed.

"So," Chad said, "you're staying the night."

"Looks like," Troy agreed.

"What do you think Raven's up to?" Chad said.

"Screwing with us."

Chad nodded. "I wish she'd leave my dad out of it."

"It'll be okay," Troy said, taking his boyfriend's hands, drawing Chad close.

Chad stood on tiptoes, lips meeting Troy's. Troy wrapped his muscular arms around Chad, kissing the top of his head. Chad pulled away, lifting his shirt over his head. Troy followed suit.

"Hey," Troy said.

"Hey," Chad echoed.

Chad grew a claw and hooked Troy's zipper, drawing it down.

"Your turn," Troy said, reaching for his boyfriend's pants. Chad pushed him away and onto the bed.

"Check this out." He backflipped; by the time he landed, Chad held his pants in one hand, socks in the other, leaving him dressed only in a pair of skimpy red underwear.

"Wow," Troy said.

"Strip," Chad ordered.

"Yes sir," Troy agreed, pushing his pants down over his thick quads.

"I'll be right back," Chad said, disappearing into the washroom.

Troy exhaled loudly, crawling under the blankets. He couldn't believe he was staying the night. He was caught between nervousness and excitement. He closed his eyes, smiling as he felt the warmth of a body under the blankets next to him. He rolled over and wrapped an arm around Chad's muscular frame. Troy's pecs pressed into the meat of the other young man's shirtless back.

Troy's hands roved up and down his boyfriend's satiny physique. Their lips met. Troy's body and mind were a swirl of sensations, and yet, underneath, something wasn't right. Their bodies, usually like puzzle pieces, didn't quite fit. The size of Chad's biceps and frame were too big, and the rhythm of their kisses was off by a beat—almost as if this weren't Chad at all.

"Troy?" Chad said from the other side of the room, standing in the doorway of the washroom, flicking on the bedroom light.

Troy pulled back in surprise, staring at Jake Kanaan blinking sleepily in his arms.

Jake jerked up in bed. "Where the hell am I?"

He gazed at Troy and toppled out of bed.

"I am so sorry," Jake blushed as he got to his feet, dressed in pajama bottoms. "Sometimes, I sleep teleport."

"Were you two making out?" Chad asked.

The red in Jake's cheeks spread to the tops of his pecs.

"He tricked me!" Troy stammered.

"I better go," Jake blurted, vanishing in a swirl of purple-pink energy.

"I can explain," Troy began. "I was lying here and...Have I mentioned how handsome you are?"

Chad's fury dissolved, replaced by a growing desire for Troy.

"Son of a…!" Chad growled, baring his fangs and pointing a claw at Troy. "You're using your power on me! Not okay."

"This wasn't my fault!" Troy said, restraining himself from using his empathic abilities on Chad. "I thought he was you!"

"That's not what I'm pissed about. That's a lie. I am pissed about you making out with Jake, but I'm more pissed about you trying to control me! That," Chad took a deep breath, hating what he was about to say, "that's what a villain would do."

Troy stepped toward him; Chad held up a hand. "You should go."

Troy pulled back, head shaking. "No way. I'm not leaving you in this house with that woman."

"Fine," Chad said. He had no desire to be left here with Raven. He grabbed the blanket from the floor and shoved it into Troy's arms. "The couch is downstairs."

"Seriously?"

"Seriously."

Troy's broad shoulders drooped. He stepped out of the bedroom then stopped, turning back to Chad.

"Keep moving, Allstar," Chad said, though a part of him wanted Troy to throw the blankets to the floor as they passionately made up.

Stop it, García, Chad ordered himself. *You're mad at him.*

"That's weird," Troy said, staring not at Chad, but through him.

Chad folded his arms over his chest.

"What's weird?" he asked. "That I'm not falling all over you for a change?"

"No," Troy said. "I could make you worship me if I wanted to. Don't get that look. If we're going to have this talk, then we're going to have this talk. Yes, Chad, I do use my powers on you. Maybe I do it too often. Maybe my good intentions aren't good enough. But part of my job as your boyfriend is to make you feel better. I *like* making you feel good. And I'm going to use everything in my power to do exactly that."

"Sometimes, you're going to have to let me feel bad," Chad said, "even if that makes *you* uncomfortable. Sometimes, that's how it is."

"What about guilt?" Troy asked. "Should I let you feel that too? Because you're feeling plenty guilty right now."

"Am not," Chad scoffed.

"Are too," Troy replied.

Now he picks up on that? Chad raged.

"What if I am?" Chad snapped. "You have no right to read my emotions."

"People read each others' moods all the time," Troy replied. "Boyfriends in particular. I just happen to be better at it than most."

"Not good enough. There needs to be rules, boundaries," Chad replied.

"How was Jake able to teleport here?" Troy asked, an edge creeping into his tone.

"He's a teleporter," Chad replied. "That's his thing."

"You said he could only teleport to places he's been before," Troy pressed.

"About that—" Chad stammered.

"He's been in your bedroom before," Troy finished for him.

"Would you believe we were study buddies?" Chad asked.

"You were in different grades," Troy replied.

"Jake…had to use the washroom when he was over for my dad's yearly football party?" Chad offered.

"He materialized in your bed," Troy countered.

Chad's jaw worked soundlessly.

"Fine, you got me," Chad said. "I don't like to talk about it because it was a mess. Jake and I have history. It ended after he graduated. That's the last time I saw him until those women attacked us at the mall. I was going to tell you, but those lesbians make everything so complicated."

"That's your excuse for not telling me?" Troy snorted.

"It's not an excuse," Chad insisted, "it just is. And it's not like you've told me everything about every girl you used to date."

"Because I wasn't into any of them," Troy said. "Do you still have feelings for Jake?"

"No!" Chad insisted. He recalled being in the malt shop, spooning rocky road into Jake's mouth.

"Liar," Troy said.

"I'm not…"

"I'm an empath," Troy said.

"But…"

"You know what?" Troy interrupted. "The couch is starting to sound like a pretty good option. I guess we both have a lot to learn about what it takes to be a hero."

Chapter 15

Raven sat crosslegged on the coach's bed; he lay next to her, snoring loudly, his spiked beer bottle beading dew on a side table. Raven stuck a round, palm-sized gadget to the wall then watched her phone take a slew of readings from Chad's room next door. At one point, she could've sworn it was detecting three lifeforms, but that couldn't be right.

Muffled arguing filtered through the thin barrier. Raven rolled her eyes. She'd handed Troy and Chad a free pass to heaven; they'd turned it into the express lane to hell. *Idiots.*

It was more confirmation that their judgment was more plugged than their pores, and they were unworthy of the powers they possessed.

She heard the door slam; Troy thud-thud-thudded his way down the stairs; she could tell it was him from the tread of his feet. Chad's was a slinking whisper. Raven's heart beat in panic.

Is Troy leaving? That would ruin the whole point of her date with Coach García.

I mean mission, she corrected herself. *This is all part of the mission.*

The "date" got her into position to get readings on Troy. But she needed him to stay. She needed him to fall asleep. She waited to hear the front door open and close, and for him to rev his bike.

How am I going to get the data we need if he leaves? she panicked. *Break into his house? Put a ladder to his window in the middle of the night? That's not suspicious. Dammit, dammit, dammit!*

But the downstairs door remained silent. Raven placed the circular device on the floor. Her phone picked up Troy's readings in the living room below.

He was staying. His breathing and heart rates slowed. *Is he sleeping on the couch? I'm rubbing that in tomorrow!*

But Y did not come before X.

Raven gazed at the readings, impatient for him to reach R.E.M. "Come on, come on…"

A smile crept at the corner of her lips as Troy's readings dipped.

"Gotch'ya."

Meanwhile, at the gay fraternity, Felix and Pixie sat at the '50s-style kitchen table with matching chairs.

"You said you were here to talk," Felix said, "so talk."

"I made a promise to you and your friends," she said, "that I would help you learn to use your powers. I'm a womyn of my word."

"Does that mean letting me read your mind so I can make sure you're telling the truth?" Felix asked.

"Sure," she shrugged.

He looked at her skeptically. She touched the metallic stone around her neck; it flared with rainbow patterns that reminded Felix of circuitry.

"That's how you're blocking me," he said, "with that."

"It's from a meteor," she explained. "It's hard to come by. The largest known fragment is sitting in a museum in France. They haven't a clue of its true value."

"How does it work?" Felix asked.

"It affects human physiology and neurology in interesting ways. If you think of the brain as a computer's hard drive, the subconscious as the operating system, a person's experiences as the programing, then this," she twisted the stone in the light, "is the firewall—and so much more."

"Are you going to take it off?" Felix asked.

Where's the fun in that? she asked.

"I heard you in my mind," he said with surprise.

"Firewalls have ways in and out—if you have the password," she said.

He considered this and went to a cupboard. "Before I was a mind reader, I was a bartender. Nothing got people to lower their guard better than this." He pulled out a bottle of tequila and poured two shots.

"I'm game," Pixie said. They clinked glasses and downed the booze. He caught a flash of a steel door in her bedroom with a weird label.

"What's Weapon XY?" he asked.

Are you sure you want to know? she replied, downing another shot. Felix played with his glass.

"It's not a what," he answered, picking up her thoughts. "His name's Caleb."

"Password Caleb accepted," she said, as if she were, in fact, a computer.

Felix felt a portion of the "firewall" within her dissolve, letting him into a deeper level. He gasped at the intensity. He was used to entering a mind like a timid swimmer dipping a toe in a pool, testing the temperature, gauging the depth, then carefully climbing down a ladder to enter incrementally. This was no pool. It was a merciless riptide that dragged him under, immersing him in Pixie's memory of a lithe young man.

At first, Felix thought it was a younger version of Raven, they looked so much alike.

This is Caleb, Felix heard Pixie's inner monologue. *He was my best friend.*

Caleb stood on a dock, sunlight dappling his skin barely concealed by tiny bathers. He smiled broadly, waving to Felix to join him. Of course, Caleb wasn't waving at Felix. Felix had never met this person or been to this cottage retreat. These were Pixie's memories. Felix saw all this through her point of view.

An '80s girly pop hit blared from a portable speaker. Felix felt himself run to Caleb, carried along the pre-laid track of Pixie's memory. Felix was there for the ride.

Caleb swept Felix-Pixie up in his arms and twirled them around. The landscape swirled, turning the horizon into a cyclone of colored inkblots. The reds, blues, and greens morphed together, and Felix was in a different memory.

The same young man was there, in a dingy bachelor apartment made brighter by yellow paint and garish curtains made of scarves that looked scavenged from someone's trash. The wild patterns framed a dirt-encrusted window that stared onto a brick wall.

Felix spied, through Pixie's eyes, plastic cockroach traps, dirty pots next to a hot plate, and a bed made from milk crates. Empty Etienne water bottles overflowed the recycling bin next to the bar fridge.

The young man—Caleb—wore tight jeans cut so low they looked like he'd raided a cowgirl's closet. His faded unicorn T-shirt showed three inches of midriff and a belly button ring glittering in candlelight.

Caleb held a birthday cake towards Felix-Pixie, the name Pixie scrawled on it in bright pink icing. Felix experienced Pixie blowing out the candles, and he heard her, the her from this memory, making a wish.

Are you surprised by what I wished for? current-day Pixie asked Felix.

As the candles went out, so too did the scene, replaced by another.

Felix found himself in a bedroom with rustic furniture made of rough wood. He lay in bed, which meant it was Pixie lying in bed. She wasn't alone. Raven was with her. Touching her. Kissing her.

"No, no," Felix said, the real Felix, back in the kitchen at the fraternity.

In the present, he tried to pull away from Pixie, sitting across from him at the kitchen table. Pixie's grip tightened on his arm. *Don't you stop,* she said. *Don't you dare. You wanted to know, so here it is—all of it.*

"I shouldn't have to see this," Felix said.

Sometimes heroes have to witness what others can't bear, Pixie replied.

The scene played faster and slower at the same time. Felix was not an empath. He couldn't feel Pixie's emotions. Still, tears came to his eyes. He was in Pixie's memory, in the bed, covered in luxurious sheets, Raven's hands all over Pixie, dressed in jeans and a bra.

The door to the bedroom opened, and Felix stared at the impossible through Pixie's eyes. Raven stood there in military fatigues. But how could that be? Here she was, also in bed with Pixie.

Does Raven have a twin sister? Felix wondered.

No, he heard Pixie reply. *She has a younger brother—Caleb.*

Military Raven in the bedroom door stared in shock at herself with her girlfriend. Pixie's head swung from the Raven in her bed to the Raven across the room, then back.

They both looked as real as real could be, but the Raven that held Pixie, the one that was in bed with her, wasn't Raven. The veil lifted; air shimmered around the false Raven, and the illusion shattered.

Felix saw what Pixie saw in that moment. He stared at Caleb entwined with Pixie's body.

"What the eff!" Raven shouted.

"I love you!" Caleb cried to Pixie, reaching for her, *"I love you like I haven't loved any man, and I know you love me too! This was your illusion, drawn from your deepest wish. We can make it real. We can be together!"*

"You've messed with our minds for the last time," Raven said, drawing her fist back and smashing him in the face.

The scene changed. Felix watched through Pixie's eyes as Raven cut the clothes from Caleb's body and lowered him into a glass cylinder with a metal base. A matching lid clicked into place, a hose attached to the top. Caleb's face was bruised, lip split, and nose crusted with blood. Raven turned a large wheel on the wall, and milky white fluid came dripping from the top of the container. It hit him like raindrops, making his eyelids flutter, and his cheek flinch. He winced, blinked rapidly at the droplets, and held a hand to shield his face.

He looked around, confusion turning to understanding, replaced by panic. He pressed his hands against the transparent cylinder. He pounded on the glass and screamed. Not a sound escaped.

Raven turned the wheel—the rain turned to a torrent. It swirled around his ankles, rising to his knees.

Please, he mouthed to Raven. *I'm your brother!* He kept banging on the soundproof material.

If Raven hadn't arrived when she did, who knows how far it would've gone, Pixie thought.

Raven grabbed hold of a thick steel door, and pushed it shut, hiding Caleb from view as the milky liquid continued past his waist. There was a whirr and clang of locks falling into place. On the steel door was stamped *WEAPON XY*.

We got the canister and vault from a millionaire scientist's estate sale, Pixie explained, releasing her hold on Felix.

He pulled back physically as he mentally withdrew from Pixie's mind. In a rush of vertigo, his psyche landed in his body with a plop. He looked around the kitchen in the gay fraternity, blinking to clear his head.

"Do you understand now?" Pixie asked.

"Caleb," Felix said, "he's your prisoner."

"He has to answer for his crimes," she said.

"He does," Felix agreed. "But us? That's how you justified attacking us? We've made some questionable decisions, but—"

She picked up the plaque.

"He didn't use to be like that either," she said. "He drank that Etienne water, and he changed. Do you get that?" There was a dangerous edge in Pixie's voice. "He *violated* me."

"He deserves a trial," Felix said. "Instead, you're holding him like a hostage."

"Do you think we want to be jail keepers? Do you think it's fun? This isn't my job. He *should* have to sit in front of a judge. But what jury could convict him? What prison could hold him? And that's the problem. Is there even a law for what he did? I thought I was having consensual relations with the woman I love. Instead, it was him, wrapped in delusion. He claims he loved me, more than he loved any man, so he cast an illusion to get what he wanted. Me. For all I know, he made me look like his latest boyband crush so that he could have his cake and screw it too. Do you have any idea how twisted that is? Do you have any clue what that did to me? To my ability to trust? To my ability to love?"

"You miss him," Felix said, catching the stray thought as the memory faded, returning his psyche to his body in the gayternity kitchen.

Present-day Pixie sat across from him, wiping a tear from her cheek. "I do," she said. "How effed up is that? The chemistry we had, it went beyond best friend. Raven used to say I loved him more than I loved her. In some ways, she was right."

Felix thought of Alejandro, but his face dissolved, replaced by Troy's.

Oh boy, Felix groaned inwardly, knowing what that meant.

"We can't sit by and see what kind of people you turn into," Pixie continued. "Your existence, you and your Queeroes, you've burned the rulebook. You can read minds, Felix. Troy can twist emotions. Who holds either of you accountable if you abuse those abilities? What constitutes abuse? I *enjoyed* being with Caleb. What do you think a misogynistic judge would do with that messed-up testimony? I don't know what to do with it. The world isn't ready for you, but, at some point, it *is* going to find out that superpowers are science fact, not fiction. When that happens, you need to be ready. You need to be above reproach. You need to be heroes because if you're villains, goddess help us all."

"And that's where you come in?" Felix challenged.

"We didn't ask for this responsibility any more than you did your powers," Pixie insisted. "But we have a moral obligation as members of the human race. I want to believe you're different from Caleb. Maybe it wasn't fully his fault. His illusions are so real, maybe he duped himself. I hope one day we can set him free. That's why I let you into my mind. You need to understand why we want to help you."

She poured another round of shots. Felix downed his, haunted by her memories and his conflicting thoughts.

"I'm sorry," he said, "for what you've been through."

"It sucks," she admitted, "but it feels better to share this with someone."

"Raven can't talk about it," Felix realized out loud. "It's too much for her. And sometimes, it's all you can talk about."

Pixie lifted the tequila bottle and took a swig. "Gold star for the mind reader."

"Relationships, am I right?" Felix asked.

She laughed and cried at the same time. So did he. "You homos and your humor," she chastised, smiling despite herself.

Thank you, she thought at him. *For staying with me to the end of that memory. For bearing witness. It helps.*

THANK YOU, he replied, FOR TRUSTING ME ENOUGH TO LET ME IN.

They clinked glasses, and Felix realized they were holding hands again. This time, it was he who had reached for her.

Chapter 16

"Thank you," Pixie said as Felix handed her a blanket and sheets. "I appreciate you letting me crash on the couch."

"Only a villain would let you drink and drive," he replied.

He pulled the living room's sliding doors closed behind him, and she listened as he walked up the stairs. When his steps grew faint, she pulled out a circular piece of tech from her satchel, stood on a chair, and stuck the gadget to the ceiling. Her phone beeped, and she gazed hungrily at the screen as it displayed Felix's biological readings.

Felix kept one steadying hand on the wall as he stumbled drunkenly along the upstairs hall.

I am going to pay for all that tequila, he smiled.

He heard the fraternity's back door open and caught Blake's thoughts as he returned home. Felix smiled at Blake's memories, sharing a fun evening with Gibbie, playing video games, and munching on popcorn. Occasionally, their shoulders had touched as they blasted space invaders.

You go, girl, Felix thought.

He reached the open door of the room he shared with Alejandro; he was passed out on the bed. A martini glass and an empty bottle of gin sat on the bedside table. Felix leaned against the doorframe, wondering if they'd still be together if not for the fact that they had these crazy powers. Being a super queer limited the dating pool. Admittedly, the phasing sex was mind-blowing.

Also, there were parts about Alejandro no one else saw, but which Felix did, like the memory of Alejandro teaching his little brother to ride a bike, of the beating Alejandro took from some neighborhood boys, and of his father grunting in a 'well what did you expect?' kind of way when he saw the black eye and split lip. Felix wiped his watery eyes, crawled drunkenly into bed, and gladly sank into oblivion.

Troy Allstar dreamed. He was at the Aberbombie and Stitch store, in a pair of ass-hugging jeans, shirtless. His name tag was pinned through his nipple. Chad was at the front of the store, greeting customers who never came. He wore the skimpiest of briefs—like he was about to enter a physique competition.

He kept spritzing PROWL at the empty air, announcing to no one, "Welcome to body-fascist central. Don't know how to feel bad about yourself? Don't worry; we'll teach you!"

Troy blinked, and Jake Kanaan appeared in a flash of lavender light. He wore his football bottoms, reminding Troy of what a star Jake had been on the team. His bare upper body bulged with muscle, his full arm tattoo glittering with rubies while his ears twinkled with huge diamond studs. Jake wrapped his strong arms around Chad, and their lips met in an equally passionate embrace. The bottle of cologne dropped from Chad's listless hand.

Troy' fist clenched in rage. *You're a dead man, Kanaan.*

ARE YOU SURE YOU WANT TO SPEND YOUR NIGHT DREAMING ABOUT THEM?

The moment Troy heard Felix's telepathic voice, he forgot about Chad and Jake. Troy turned, and there was Felix, as solid as solid could be. He stood next to a display of perfectly arranged crewnecks. In this dream, Felix looked so much like Jesse; it hurt.

"It's good to see y—" Felix began.

Troy grabbed Felix, kissing him furiously.

When Troy awoke, he sat upright on the couch and gazed around the García living room. His body dripped with sweat, and his mind burned with the memory of what he and Felix had done.

Troy flushed guiltily. *It was just a dream*, he reassured himself. Technically, that was true, yet what he'd experienced was beyond intimate. *We shared a dream. Who does that?*

Whatever Troy might tell himself, it had been real in its own way. Felix had been there, in his mind, or he'd been inside Felix's—or both. Troy's body hummed from the experience.

Does this mean I cheated on Chad? No, Troy assured himself. Whatever it was that had happened, it was still a dream. If he'd been awake, he never would've kissed Felix, or touched him, or…

The memories made Troy adjust himself. *Maybe I would.*

He still felt Felix's lips on his, smooth yet firm. *Like Jesse's.*

Troy tensed.

Felix isn't his brother, Troy reminded himself. *Jesse's dead, and I love Chad, right?*

After last night's fight with his boyfriend, Troy wondered. He'd felt powerless finding out about Jake. Chad made a fool of him. Jake was probably laughing his ass off.

The thought dimmed when Troy thought about Felix. *We had dream sex. Am I still a virgin?*

"Yes," he assured himself. "That did not count. Chad will be my first."

But will I be Chad's?

That morning, in the gay-ternity, steam filled a washroom, the water as hot as Felix could stand. He sanded his skin with a fuchsia loofah and a scented body wash. His head ached from the tequila. The emotional hangover was worse. His underwear, with its telltale evidence of his and Troy's nocturnal adventure, was buried at the bottom of the hamper.

It didn't really happen, it didn't really happen, it didn't really happen, Felix assured himself over and over. *It was ridiculously hot, though!*

When he kissed Troy, Felix experienced what Troy experienced, and vice versa. It was a sensate feedback loop, exploding in a kaleidoscope of psychedelic wonder that made this dimension feel like a dying black hole. By comparison, phasing sex was the clumsiest of masturbation.

The shower door slid open, and Felix's naked boyfriend joined him in the stall. Alejandro's smooth muscles flexed and relaxed as he lathered them in suds. "Get my back, babe," he said.

"Sure," Felix said, grabbing a bar of soap. *I can do this*, he assured himself. *He's my boyfriend. Sometimes, I don't like him, but I do love him.*

Taking a breath, Felix pressed the bar of soap over his boyfriend's back and stopped.

"What the hell?" Felix said.

"What's up?" Alejandro asked, rinsing the shampoo from his hair.

"I think we have a problem," Felix said.

Alejandro turned. Felix reached for him, and his hand went through Alejandro's chest.

Alejandro's eyes widened in surprise. "Cojeme," he swore.

"You're not doing that?" Felix asked.

Alejandro shook his head. He reached for Felix, and Alejandro's hand passed through as if his boyfriend weren't there. Panic filled Alejandro's watery eyes. "Am I turning into a ghost?" He leaned against the tile wall for support. It held him up, solid as could be. He picked up a bottle of conditioner, squirted some into his hand, and dragged it through his hair without a problem.

"Not a ghost," he said with relief. He tried caressing Felix's cheek. Alejandro's hand phased through his boyfriend. "So why can't I touch you?"

Meanwhile, at Nuffim High, bright yellow school buses pulled in and out of the institution's cracked parking lot.

"I'd have sex with She-Ra, kill Evil-Lyn, and marry Shadow Weaver," Matt said to Carl and Gibbie as they got off a bus.

"She *is* badass," Gibbie agreed. He wore a T-shirt with Sir Ian McKellan on it, along with the words, *I'm Magneto and Gandalf. Get over it.*

"Speaking of Screw, Marry, Kill," Matt said, stopping abruptly, "I think Gibbie's about to have a dating life."

"What's that supposed to…" Gibbie's words trailed off.

"Impressive," Carl said, his mouth awash with latte. He took another slurp.

Gibbie stared at Blake dressed in full steampunk attire. He wore an Abraham Lincoln glue-on beard with matching hat, a black tuxedo with a bulky puffed out crimson tie, a floral corset around his belly, leather-bound flying goggles perched on his forehead, an antique-style jetpack strapped to his back, and, holstered to his hip, a pistol that looked both futuristic and archaic.

Matt whistled, "Wow."

"Shut up," Gibbie said. Blake clutched a bouquet of dried roses. Gibbie's mouth ran dry.

"Good luck, dude," Matt clapped him on the back.

"Guys," Gibbie said. "Guys?"

They left him alone under Blake's worshipful stare.

Gibbie wiped his sweaty palms on his jeans.

"Hey Blake," he said, voice cracking.

"These are for you," Blake said, thrusting the flowers at him.

"Thanks," Gibbie said, accepting them and smiling nervously. "Cool outfit."

"You like it? I love the whole technology meets wild west motif, you know?"

"Sure. So we're friends, right?" Gibbie offered, hoping Blake would catch his drift and take the out.

"We could be more than friends," Blake said.

"I don't want to be more than friends," Gibbie blurted.

Before Blake could answer, a swirl of purple-pink energy erupted between them, vomiting out Jake's muscular form. He staggered into a dumpster. He wore jeans and a "Let's Rock" T-shirt with bolts of lightning blasting outward. The sides were cut out, showing off his flanks. He leaned against the rusting bin, panting.

"Jake?" Gibbie asked. "You okay?"

"Hey, Gibbie," Jake wheezed. "Is Chad here?"

"No," Gibbie said.

"We used to come here sometimes," Jake said wistfully, clutching at his abs as if he had the worst cramp of his life.

"Right," Gibbie said, "back when you two were...involved."

There was a catch to Gibbie's voice as he said it.

"Ancient history," Jake said, dripping sweat. "I should probably..." Jake jerked his thumb towards the school, and he was gone in wisps of pink energy.

"It's because I'm fat, isn't it?" Blake said.

"What?" Gibbie asked. "You shouldn't use that word."

"Why? Because it makes you uncomfortable? That's why you're not interested in me—because I don't look like Jake, who you're infatuated with, or Chad, who was your obsession."

Blake's eyes filled with tears. Another bus pulled into the lot, gears grinding, followed by the squeals of high schoolers disembarking. Gibbie blushed as people pointed and laughed at Blake.

"I collected these flowers two years ago, growing wild," Blake said. "I told myself I'd give them to the first worthy guy I met. I thought that was you. I was wrong." Blake threw the dried roses in Gibbie's face.

"Blake—"

"Screw you! You're as shallow as the rest of them. You're a villain!" Blake yelled, storming off and wiping the tears from his eyes.

Gibbie picked up the flowers.

You're a villain, Blake's words echoed.

Gibbie knew what it felt like to have the object of his affection reject him. Now the rejected had become the rejector; the victim now the victimizer. He wished the lesbians would make a move. He'd rather deal with them than this.

His conflicting emotions churned harder. His fist clenched, and he punched a hole through the dumpster.

Nearby, Mandy sat in class, blowing a bubble of pink gum, tapping her heel against the floor and smacking her pencil against her books.

Markham sat in front of her. He whipped around and slammed his hand on her desk. "That is annoying."

Mandy popped her bubble and stabbed her pencil at his hand. He barely jerked back in time to avoid being skewered.

Troy and Chad entered the class together.

"Oh look," Markham smirked, "it's your butt-pirate ex and the fruity friend you wish you could marry."

Usually, Troy and Chad were snuggle bugs. Today, not so much. Pixie stood at the front of the class, a knowing smile on her lips as she appraised them.

"I'll be filling in today," Pixie said as the last of the students took their seats. "I understand you've been reading the *Chrysalids*. It's the story of eight telepaths who have to keep their abilities a secret. There are three boys and five girls. And while they are deviants, they are heteronormative deviants. You're a romantic Mandy. What does that mean for two of the girls?"

"It means," Mandy said, "they would have to marry norms, or not at all."

"One of the telepaths does marry a norm. How does that work out for her?" Pixie asked.

"She kills herself," Markham answered.

Pixie nodded, gazing at Mandy meaningfully.

"Sucks to be her," Mandy shrugged, pretending not to get the implication that as the token girl with powers, she would never find a guy with powers to be with and would share the same fate as the doomed character in question.

"The cheerleader feigned indifference," Pixie said, as if narrating a play, "fooling no one."

"I get it!" Markham perked up, turning to face Mandy. "You're like the girl in the book. You're going to die pathetic and alone—because you surround yourself with gay guys who will never love you."

He didn't have all the pieces, but he had enough to solve the puzzle. Mandy turned her pencil invisible and stabbed it into the back of his hand. He screamed, toppled out of his chair, and thudded onto his butt. He stared at the writing implement protruding between two knuckles. He jerked it out and clutched the bloody hole.

"How demented are you?" he demanded.

"Ms. Kim!" Pixie shouted. "Detention, after school."

"Why?" Mandy snorted. "For sticking up for myself? Not very feminist AF of you."

"You can't afford to give in to your emotions. Not like this. You have to be better than him," Pixie replied.

"I am better than him," Mandy said. "And I'm better than you." She slid her books into her handbag, slung it over her shoulder, picked up her purse, and got out of her seat.

"What do you think you're doing?" Pixie asked.

"I'm not sure how you and your friends got these jobs," Mandy snipped, "but you're not actually our teacher." With that, she cat-walked out of the room. The rest of the students gaped, all except Markham. He shoved his books into his knapsack and tossed it over his shoulder.

"Et tu?" Pixie asked.

"I need a bandage," Markham replied, holding up his injured hand. Someone threw a tampon at him. It smacked Markham's face and fell to his feet.

"Ha, ha," he said, and he followed Mandy out the door.

In the hallway, Markham had every intention of going to the nurse's office—and then dicking around for the rest of the period. Maybe he could find some nerds to harass. First, he needed to get in one last dig with Mandy; otherwise, she'd think he'd gone soft. He opened his lips, an epic put down at the ready. He looked both ways. The hall was empty.

"Man, I hate her," Markham said. He leaned against some lockers and began typing her a scathing text; a muffled sob stopped him. He searched the empty hall. The air shimmered, and there was Mandy, on the floor, knees hugged to her chest.

"Am I high?" he asked.

"Yes," she said.

"I don't remember smoking up," he said.

She rolled her eyes. "Enjoy the view. Here I am, at my worst. Best day ever for you."

It should've been, but her pointing it out to him, rather than the other way around, stole the air from his balloon.

"All right, let's hear it," she said. "Tell my ovaries how they're going to dry up while I turn into a lonely cat lady."

"You read my mind," Markham lied. Truth was, Mandy's self-deprecation made his taunts feel weak. "You're crazy, you know that, right?" he asked. His tone was more friendly than accusatory—like he was commenting on a bold-but-questionable fashion accessory. "Like, scary crazy."

She looked at the blood drying around the puncture she'd made near his middle finger.

"You should disinfect that," she said. She took a travel bottle of liquid sanitizer from her purse. She squirted a dollop onto the wound, rubbing in the disinfectant with one fingertip.

He considered making a crude comment. *Keep your stupid mouth shut for once*, he advised himself.

"There," she said. He helped her to her feet. She smoothed out her skirt.

"You have any lipstick and eyeliner?" he asked.

She arched a confused brow. "You turning trans on me, O'Reilly?"

He rolled his eyes.

"Okay," she said, "I'll play."

She handed him the makeup, and he cupped her chin.

"You made a mess of yourself with all your crying," he explained. To her surprise, he refreshed her makeup with expert hands. Chad had done this for her before, but her heart never beat this quickly at her friend's touch.

"I had a camp counselor who was into this," Markham explained, applying concealer, lipstick, and eyeshadow. "She was whack. Good kisser, though." He appraised his work. "Better," he said, his lips full and lush.

"Thanks," Mandy said as he placed the makeup back in her hand. She felt weirdly jealous of the girl who taught him how to do this; grateful, too.

She gave his fingers a gentle squeeze. He squeezed back.

"Mandy, can I—" he started.

"Yes," she replied.

He pulled her into his body. It was nice to be held instead of being smothered by Troy and Chad's PDAs with each other or Pixie's tales of Mandy's romantic doom.

I'll show her, Mandy thought as Markham's lips met hers.

She'd expected him to be a tongue monster, but he took it slow, free-styling with nibbles and strategic tongue darts. His camp counselor had taught him well.

"Mandy," he breathed into her ear; she thrilled at the sound of her name vibrating up from his broad chest. Ever since she got these powers, she'd felt more and more alone, the future morphing into a maw of uncertainty. Getting it on with self-proclaimed "manslut" Markham was foolish, but oh the relief to feel enveloped, to be free of uncertainty, if only temporarily.

"Markham," she whispered, *you stupidly hot jackass.*

"Mandy..."

She grew hotter, her kisses more fervent. She pressed him against the lockers. She expected him to be a fumbling fool, groping clumsily and ready to spooge his pants at her slightest touch. Instead, his hands roved slowly and expertly over her body. Her thermostat jumped another three notches.

She leaned into him. He stroked her hair as she nuzzled into his chest, kissing the exposed top of his pecs. He did a quick turn, flipping her around to press her into the lockers; his size and strength wrapped about her. His arms were a shield that, for once, she didn't have to generate herself. The warmth in her grew stronger. His mouth found hers again.

Her skin sizzled. She ignored the sweat at the base of her back and pulled his muscled form into hers. It had been so long, she'd forgotten how wonderful this could be.

"Goddamn, you're a furnace," he said, his bedroom eyes making her broil. She yanked off his letterman jacket, her nails raking along his biceps.

The fire in her body scorched through her, desperate for release.

"More!" she said, though a part of her whispered, *something's wrong.*

Her lips were all over his; the pressure in her grew; she guided his hand under her shirt, moving it up her stomach to rove over her bra—and with a boom, her forcefield exploded outwards, sending him flying from her arms to slam with a loud CRUNCH against the lockers, his body imprinting the metal before curdling unconscious to the floor.

She stared in shock. "Markham?"

His head lolled to one side. A trickle of blood dribbled from an ear.

Door after door along the corridor slammed open. With a sharp intake of breath, Mandy wrapped herself in invisibility.

Teachers rushed towards Markham. Students held themselves back inside classroom doorways. Chad's nostrils flared. He stared at Mandy. Invisibility didn't fool his sense of smell. Pixie followed Chad's gaze then typed madly on her phone. Mandy heard the bling of a text message.

For a moment, a cell phone appeared to float in the middle of the hall, turning visible so she could read it. On the glowing screen was condemnation framed in a blue bubble.

Mandy Kim, what have you done? 😨

Chapter 17

Mandy stood outside the school, staring at Markham on a gurney, paramedics loading him into an ambulance. They strapped an oxygen mask to his mouth; an IV bag dripped a clear liquid into his veins. Chad stood next to Mandy.

"What are they saying?" she asked.

"Broken arm and leg, cracked ribs, possible internal bleeding," Chad replied, his keen hearing catching every word.

"I didn't mean to," Mandy said.

"What happened?" Chad asked.

"I...we...we were—"

"Audible gasp!" Chad clutched his chest. "Were you macking on Markham? Gurl!"

The paramedics slammed the doors of the ambulance and drove off, sirens blaring. Mandy twisted her purse.

"So," Chad said, putting a comforting arm around her shoulder, "does this mean he was really good or really bad?"

"Chad!" she smacked him away. "Markham's being taken to the hospital, and it's my fault."

Chad waited for an answer.

"He was amazing," she said in a hushed tone, glancing around to make sure no one else heard.

"How good?" Chad said from the side of his mouth.

"Out of 10, he's a 12," Mandy said.

"Wow," Chad nodded. "Maybe I should kiss him."

"Hands off, García."

"Mandy Kim, are you in love?" Chad asked.

"Puh-lease," Mandy scoffed. "Markham's a tool. It was purely physical. Like, *primal*. I've never felt anything like it. My body literally exploded."

"Well," Chad said, his yes drifting to the phone in his hand. "This is the first time you've made out with a guy since, you know, the change."

Mandy gave him cut-eye. "This isn't menopause. Are you texting Troy in the middle of my crisis?"

Chad pressed send and shoved his phone into his pocket. "Sorry, girl, we're fighting. But I'm here for you, one-hundred perc—" His phone bleeped. "Eighty-three percent," Chad corrected. "I'm here for you eighty-three percent."

"Just check the text," Mandy said. "At least, if you're fighting, you know Troy's not using his powers to control you."

"Yeah," Chad replied. "Is it bad that I kind of wish he would? This feeling sucks."

Mandy nodded, watching as Raven emerged from the school, marching towards her Hummer. "Le sigh," Mandy said, staring at Raven. "I can't believe I'm about to do this. Chad, I'll catch you later."

"Sure," Chad said, typing on his phone. "Wait, Mandy, where are you going?"

He watched Mandy reach Raven's side.

"Am I next on your hit list?" the tall woman asked. She folded her arms over her muscular chest, bunching the folds of her tracksuit. "Or does sending one person to the hospital fill your quota for the day?"

Mandy's jaw jutted, but she was out of quips. Her eyes watered. She hated it when that happened. "It was an accident."

"Accidents can be avoided," Raven replied.

"You said you were here to help," Mandy said. "Can you? Can you help me be in control?"

Raven waited for the count of five heartbeats. The delay had the desired effect.

"Please?" Mandy added.

"Yes," Raven said at last, "yes, I can."

Chad moved to block Mandy as she asked Raven for help. Instead, he ran into a swirl of purple-pink energy. He bounced off Jake's hunky form as it materialized in front of him. Chad landed in the crab position, gazing up at his ex. Jake looked ready to say something, probably another stupid apology.

Chad hopped to his feet and held up his hand.

"Not a word."

Jake watched as Chad turned about and marched back into the school, yanking his phone from his pocket to read a text message from Mandy.

Don't come after me. I need help. Let them help me if they can.

Chad gnashed his jaw, typing back.

Jake is stalking me. VILLAIN 😾*!*

Chad pressed send as he entered the school, turning into the boys' washroom. He went into a stall, dropped his pants, and tried to sit on the toilet. His backside landed on Jake's lap.

Chad gazed at the ceiling, speaking to the dried pink gum that was stuck there.

"That better be a banana-shaped cell phone in your pants, Jake Kanaan."

Chad didn't wait for a reply. He stood, pulled his underwear and pants on, and folded his biceps over his chest, staring at his ex seated on the toilet.

"This is too weird," Chad said.

"You think I don't know that?" Jake snapped. "I don't even know how I knew you would be here."

Chad held up his hand. "One way or another, we're putting an end to this tired plotline."

Meanwhile, Mandy was determined to rewrite her own out-of-control narrative. She sat cross-legged on a wrestling mat in the middle of the gym, hands resting on her knees in classic Buddha pose. Surrounding her was a circle of football blocking dummies. Their metal frames were rusting skeletons, weighed down by multiple 45-pound plates.

Raven stood inside the door of the girls' change room.

"Close your eyes, take a deep breath, and as you exhale, allow a wave of relaxation to wash from the top of your head to the bottoms of your feet," Raven said in a surprisingly melodic tone. Mandy did as she was told, breathing deeply.

"As you continue to breathe," Raven said, "relaxing more with each breath, imagine yourself at the top of a staircase. I will count from ten to one, and with each count, you will take a step down; with every step, you will relax more and more. Let's begin with ten..."

At the same time, in a nearby school hallway…

"Come on," Chad said, shoving Jake past dented lockers. Chad's phone beeped—another message from Troy.

Waiting for you at my bike 😺🐱 🍴.

All Chad wanted was to mend fences with his man then melt in his arms. But the back of Jake's shapely frame caught his eye.

Are you sure that's all you want? he asked himself. *Are you sure Troy's the one for you?*

Focus, García, he ordered himself.

Gonna run some track, he typed hastily. Troy was an empath, but he couldn't catch lies via text. *Want to make things better though* 😔. *See you tonight?*

"Nine," Raven said to Mandy in the gym, "stepping deeper into relaxation..."

Troy leaned against his motorbike, waiting for the usual lightning-quick response from Chad. When it came, Troy crinkled his brow and felt a pang as he saw that Chad wanted to run laps. Though Troy often felt like they needed space, he preferred it to be on his terms.

Take it easy, Allstar, he told himself. *We'll sort this out.*

He forgot the text the moment he saw Felix and Alejandro walking out of the school together. Troy flushed guiltily as he met Felix's eye, and he felt a wave of desire wash off the handsome youth. Alejandro instinctively reached for Felix's hand; oddly it passed right through. There was a frustrated set to Alejandro's jaw and his eyes were bloodshot.

"Eight," Raven told Mandy, watching the girl's eyelids flutter.

"Where are we going?" Jake asked Chad.

"To see Pixie. I doubt she'll be of any use, but at this point I'm despera—"

Jake whipped around, grabbed Chad's smooth forearm, and pulled him in tight.

"What are you—" Chad protested.

Purple-pink energy erupted from every sinew and cell of Jake's bod, wrapping them in a blanket of warmth. There was a stomach-churning sense of dislocation, like the exhilarating drop of a roller coaster, and they rematerialized inside Pixie's office.

She didn't blink at their arrival, typing on her computer, pausing one hand to hold up a finger for silence. With a final click of her mouse, she turned to them. "You're late."

"Seven, another step, and six, deeper and deeper..." Raven said hypnotically.

"Weird day, huh?" Troy asked, looking from Felix to Alejandro, then back to Felix.

"Is that Markham kid going to be okay?" Felix asked.

"He's a douche, but yeah, he's tough," Troy answered.

They fell silent. All Troy wanted was to press his lips to Felix's.

Stop it! Troy commanded himself. *I'm with Chad.*

"We should get going," Alejandro said, reaching for Felix; again, his hand slid through his boyfriend. Alejandro flexed his fingers in frustration.

"Yeah, me too, I'm pretty beat," Troy agreed. "I think I'll go home and take a nap."

Troy's eyes met Felix's.

"Yeah," Felix agreed, "a nap sounds good."

"What is up with you and naps these days?" Alejandro said. "When did that become such a thing?"

Troy and Felix exchanged guilty looks.

"I should—" Felix indicated over his shoulder.

"Yup," Troy agreed, giving a giant yawn and arm stretch that pulled his shirt up and revealed his lower abs.

"...and four," Raven intoned. "Almost there..."

As Mandy tranced out, Raven walked around, attaching what looked like a black metal marble behind each football dummy. They stuck like magnets.

Chad and Jake each sat on an uncomfortable wooden chair facing Pixie.

"So, Jake keeps teleporting uncontrollably," Pixie said.

"Exactly," Jake said.

"Places where you and Chad had intimate relations," Pixie pressed.

Jake blushed. "That about sums it up."

"I can help you," Pixie said. "But first," she held up a finger as they leaned forward, "you're going to get me this."

She swiveled her computer monitor to show them the image of a chunk of metallic black rock.

"What is that?" Jake asked.

"Something that was taken from an Algonquin First Nation," Pixie replied. "We're going to repatriate it. Think of yourselves as Robin Hood and his *very* merry men. Oh, and you're going to need Gibbie. It's heavy."

"Three," Raven murmured to Mandy, whose head was slumped to her chest, hands wilted onto the mat at her side.

When Troy got home, he ran upstairs and threw himself onto his bed. "Why am I doing this?" he asked himself.

He didn't wait for an answer. He closed his eyes and drifted away. As he succumbed to sleep, he dreamed he was in the boy's locker room back at school. He wore his wrestling singlet, the feel of the fabric tight on his muscular body, his pecs bursting out on either side of the straps.

"Hey, handsome."

Troy turned at the sound of Felix's voice. He wore skin-hugging jeans, high-top sneakers, and no shirt. "Hey, mister," Troy said and took Felix into his arms, their lips pressing together.

"Two..." Raven intoned, gazing at the metal objects placed on the backs of the football dummies.

There was a swirl of pink energy, and when it dissipated, Gibbie, Chad, and Jake stared at the marbled muscle of Michelangelo's *Dying Slave*.

"Welcome to Paris," Jake said.

"...and one... stepping into the basement of relaxation," Raven said. "Now feel that feeling you had, right before Markham was injur—"

Mandy inhaled sharply, fists clenched. Her head jerked back, mouth open, and her pulsing blue force shield burst outward. It smashed into the football tackling dummies and sent them flying into the walls.

Raven ducked to avoid a 45lbs plate. It stuck in the wall, vibrating. She stared at the football dummies strewn about like a trailer park after a hurricane.

One might expect fury, disappointment, or awe from the woman whose new protégé had failed to show the slightest control.

Instead, Raven looked hungrily at the metal marbles she'd attached to the football dummies. Each of them glowed with blue circuitry, pulsing like Mandy's forcefield. Raven smiled.

Mandy opened her eyes, pouting at the devastation. "Should I try again?"

Raven pulled one of the metal marbles off the back of a dummy, careful to keep it hidden from Mandy's view. "I think that's enough for one day."

Chapter 18

Jake, Chad, and Gibbie all wore black hoodies, drawn to hide their faces. Chad had cut off his sleeves. He felt very *Mission Impossible*. They gazed at Michelangelo's *Dying Slave*. His perfect curls, lean muscles, and pouty expression could have landed him an Aberbombie modeling contract.

Gibbie held a museum map. "This way," he pointed to the left.

"Pixie says she's disabled the internal alarms and put security cameras on a loop," Jake said as they stopped in front of a door leading to another wing. "Place is locked tight, though."

Gibbie nudged the door with his super strength; it popped open.

"Easy squeezy," Chad said, stepping through to stop in front of a pair of security guards staring at them in open-mouthed shock.

"Sorry about this," Chad said.

The guards went for their guns. Chad was all over them with animalistic speed, strength, and agility, unleashing a series of kicks and punches. They dropped to the ground, weapons still holstered.

"Chop chop," he said, waving for Gibbie and Jake to hurry up.

Chad took out a dozen guards by the time they reached the geological wing.

"There it is," Chad pointed at a chunk of black metallic rock the size of a basketball.

"Do you think it's as heavy as Pixie says?" Jake asked.

Chad shrugged, gripping it with both hands. The striations in his chest stood out between the half-open zipper of his hoodie, but the rock stayed put.

"Let me," Gibbie snorted, picking it up with one hand and tucking it under his arm. "Shall we?"

"How much of a rush are you guys to get back to Nuffim?" Jake asked. Before anyone could answer, pink energy erupted from him; an instant later, they were high above the ground, staring out over the Parisian night sky.

Chad smiled in childish wonder. "We're on the effing Eiffel Tower!"

"I promised I'd bring you here someday," Jake said. "I keep my word, even if it takes a while." Jake teleported away, reappearing with a bottle of champagne. He popped the cork and poured three glasses.

"Here's to settling the past so we can move onto the future," Jake said.

The trio of thieves clinked glasses.

By the second glass, Gibbie was eyeing Chad and Jake, who were laughing easily and leaning in close. Chad noticed Gibbie noticing, and before Troy's brother could say anything, Chad asked, "So what's the deal with you and Blake?"

Gibbie held out his glass for a refill. Jake obliged.

"He asked me out. I said no. That's the short version."

"Not your type?" Chad asked, noticing how Gibbie eyed Jake's biceps.

"I like him," Gibbie said. "I just don't like him like him. Does that make me a horrible person?"

Jake shrugged. "We're guys. We can be A-holes."

"I'll say," Chad said, eyeing Jake meaningfully. Chad held up a finger before Jake could say anything. "One trip to the Eiffel Tower does not make up for treating me like a disposable squeeze toy, teleporting into my bed, and making out with my boyfriend."

"Troy gets to make out with everyone!" Gibbie gaped. "So not fair. Ugh. Maybe I should've said yes to Blake. I mean, I've never even been on a gay date."

"Have you been on a straight date?" Chad asked.

"Not the point," Gibbie replied, pouring himself more champagne.

"Well, call him. Ask him out. See what happens," Chad suggested.

"But what if it goes bad?" Gibbie asked. "What if he goes for the kiss? What if he doesn't go for the kiss?"

"If you don't try, you'll never know. Even if Blake's not the love of your life, you may end up with some pretty special experiences out of it," Chad argued. Jake raised an eyebrow at that. "Don't make this about you," Chad chastised his ex.

"So, I call him, right now?" Gibbie asked.

"Pretty much," Chad said.

Gibbie considered this. "Okay, sure, why not?" he asked, sounding a bit drunk. Whether it was from the liquid courage or the regular kind, he pulled out his phone and stepped to the other side of the viewing platform.

Normally, Chad would hear every word, but as he leaned on the guardrail and admired the rising sun, Jake's body casually brushed against him. Chad didn't move away.

"Sunrise on the Eiffel Tower," Chad said, taking a break from the champagne to drink in the experience. "It's not the worst." He leaned into Jake, looking up at him, lips parted. Jake's mouth moved towards his—

"Guys!" Gibbie screeched. Chad and Jake jerked away from each other. Gibbie did a victory dance. "Blake said yes!"

Jake high-fived him. Gibbie picked Chad up and twirled him around.

"And now I'm dizzy," Gibbie said, setting Chad down to lean on his knees. "Deep breaths."

Chad and Jake smiled; when they looked at each other, there was no hint of an impending kiss. The moment had passed.

The band of merry—and tipsy—men rematerialized in Pixie's school office. Sunrise in Paris was the middle of the night in Nuffim. Pixie sat at her desk, gazing through a pair of high-tech goggles at what looked like a large marble; it was a shiny blue, not unlike Mandy's forcefield. A black-and-white portrait of Madame Curie watched from the wall. Pixie gazed up as they appeared, set the marble with a matching set, all of them shiny blue, and removed her eye ware.

"Here it is," Gibbie said, setting the shiny black rock onto her desk with a thud. "When are we handing it over to its rightful owners?"

"Soon," she said evasively. "I need to take a small sample for my research."

Jake picked up one of the marbles. A dozen of them rested on indented foam padding. "What kind of research?" he asked.

"Some new tech I'm puttering on," she answered. "The structural composition of this element is unique. The way it affects brainwaves could have major implications for mental health. It also absorbs certain wavelengths of energy."

Jake raised a shapely brow. "It didn't affect my teleports."

She waved that away. "Your power operates on a quantum spectrum. With a little ingenuity from me," she held up one of the glowing orbs she was working on, "that meteor could end humanity's reliance on fossil fuels, among other breakthroughs."

"How does it work?" Gibbie asked.

"The short version is, its crystalline matrix is programable and can interface with organics," Pixie said. "I take a small piece of it, put it inside a containment orb, and—"

"Cool stuff happens," Jake concluded.

"Precisely," Pixie agreed.

"I read about something like that," Gibbie said. "A team in Australia uploaded computer code to crystals and manipulated their growth patterns."

"Imagine if we could upload other commands or download crystalline structural matrixes," Pixie said, her eyes afire with scientific fervor.

"Never mind that," Chad interrupted, not understanding a word of her tech talk. "You said you could help Jake with his stalker problem."

"I'm fairly certain I already have," Pixie replied.

"How do you figure that?" Chad demanded.

"The more you pushed Jake away, the more he kept coming back," she explained. "Tonight, you had to work as a team. You had to let him in, with boundaries. That's the key to any good relationship."

"That's not good enou—" Chad started to say.

Jake yawned. "Maybe she's right. Maybe that together time was what we needed. And if she's wrong, we take the rock back. It's not like she can stop us."

Pixie's face puckered at his words.

"I feel better," Jake insisted. "Really."

"And if you sleep teleport into my bed again?" Chad asked.

"Be gentle when you kick me out," Jake winked.

Chad glared at Pixie. "You're ruining my life; you know that, right?"

"I think you'll find your life is about to change," she replied.

"Whatever," Chad said, putting a hand on Jake's shoulder. "I have a boyfriend to make up with. Come on Gibbie."

Gibbie happily grasped Jake's biceps, and they were gone in a burst of flamingo luminescence. The moment she was alone, Pixie called out.

"You can come in now!"

The wooden door to the hall creaked open. Raven strode in, followed by Blake. He had to wiggle to get through the entry.

"Are you sure now's the best time?" Blake asked.

"Do you want to be at your best for your date with Gibbie?" Pixie asked.

"Maybe he doesn't care that—"

"You're obese?" Raven asked.

Blake gave her a dark look. "This was a mistake."

"I'm sure Gibbie sees you for the wonderful person you are," Pixie said.

"Or he's a chubby chaser," Raven added with intentional cruelty.

"It's also possible Gibbie's being nice because he feels bad for hurting your feelings. You did lay on a pretty heavy guilt trip when he rejected you. Or maybe you're the one who's afraid. Maybe you're afraid to lose the weight, because what if you do, and you go on a date with Gibbie, and he's still not interested? No hiding behind excuses then, is there?"

Blake stared at the floor. Pixie jerked her head at Raven. The tall woman took out a sledgehammer and smashed it against the museum rock. A piece the size of a fingernail splintered off.

"What is that?" Blake asked.

"A gift from space," Pixie said.

"It's a meteor?" Blake asked.

"One of a kind," Pixie replied. She picked up the sliver of space rock and placed it on her e-pad. "We've been studying your abilities. I have to upload the necessary command sequences and..." The rock flashed with rainbow circuitry, and the e-pad pinged, "*Voila!*"

Pixie took Blake's hand and placed the cold metallic chunk in his palm, closing his fingers over it.

He shivered. "It's cold."

"It's absorbing your ambient heat, but that's a fraction of what it can do," Pixie said. "Your power is constantly absorbing energy from the world around you, which your body stores as fat. You're getting fatter as we speak. To reverse the process, you need a way of safely discharging that energy."

"Into this?" Blake asked.

"Let 'er rip," Raven said.

Blake took a deep breath; as he exhaled, his brow furrowed, and the crackling red energy erupting around his hand was sucked into the extraterrestrial stone. He gasped and pulled at the waistband of his pants. It gave an inch. "I can't believe it. I've lost weight."

The piece of rock in his hand pulsed red in the pattern of circuitry. "Put it in here," Pixie said, "or your body will just reabsorb the power." She held an open metal sphere. Blake placed the glowing rock inside; Pixie snapped it shut. The orb was a shiny blue, in a shade similar to Mandy's shield.

Raven broke off another chunk of the meteor and handed it to Blake.

"Again," Pixie said.

Blake channeled another round of energy into the black metallic rock. It flared with demonic colors, reflecting in Pixie's green eyes. The stone around her neck flickered in unison with an inner light.

"From a little spark," Pixie said, quoting Dante's *The Inferno* as she closed another shiny blue sphere around a pulsating meteor shard, "may burst a flame."

110

Chapter 19

A swirl of purple-pink energy illuminated Gibbie's backyard, depositing Gibbie, Chad, and Jake next to Troy's motorbike. There was a quietness to them, and not simply from exhaustion. They'd shared an adventure on the other side of the world; now, they were returning to reality in Nuffim.

"Well, I guess I should head," Jake said.

"Right," Chad agreed. "Are we good?"

"Yeah," Jake said. "I think we are. I feel different. Settled. Maybe those lesbians knew what they were talking about."

"Good night, Jake," Chad said.

"Thanks for an awesome night." With a wave, Jake disappeared in a swirl of energy.

"So is everything cool between the two of you?" Gibbie asked.

"It's getting there," Chad said. "Would you mind if I came in to see Troy? I don't want any secrets between us, and it should be me who tells him we all went to Paris."

They entered the dark house, and Chad used his feline night vision to lead them up the stairs.

"G'night," Gibbie whispered as he opened his bedroom door.

"G'night," Chad whispered back, slipping into Troy's room.

Chad made out the silhouette of his man in bed. Troy moaned.

"Frisky," Chad whispered, bending to kiss Troy's ear.

"Oh, Felix," Troy groaned. Chad froze. "I love you, Felix."

"Oh, hells no," Chad said, grabbing Troy's shoulders and shaking them violently.

"Yes, Felix, yes!" Troy said, still asleep.

Chad slapped him. "Wake up!"

Troy kept sleeping. Chad's eyes narrowed. Troy was an empath. Felix was a telepath. Could that mean…

"This better not be what I think it is," Chad said. He pulled out his phone and made a call. "Jake, it's Chad. Now that we're besties, I have a favor to ask."

Chad was pretty sure that his plan landed him squarely inside the axis of villainy, but he had his jealous-boyfriend get-into-jail-free card, and he was cashing it in.

So it was that Jake and he materialized hand-in-hand in a swirl of pink energy in the kitchen of the gayternity.

"You sure you want to do this?" Jake asked.

Chad pulled his hand free. "I have to know for sure."

Chad sniffed the air and marched to the front hall. He jumped back as Alejandro dropped down through the ceiling.

The handsome youth's face contorted with tearful rage.

"You keep your slut boyfriend away from my man!" he shouted. Before Chad could answer, Alejandro stormed out of the house, phasing through the door. They heard the skidding of tires on gravel. Jake held up his hands to Chad.

"I'm sure there's an explan—"

Chad swung over the banister and raced up the stairs on all fours. He slammed open the door to Felix's room.

Felix lay in a king-sized bed, fast asleep. "Troy," he moaned.

Chad's eyes streamed tears.

"That doesn't prove anyth—," Jake said.

"But it does," Chad replied. "I don't know how they're doing what they're doing, but they are."

"They're just dreaming," Jake offered.

"That makes it worse," Chad sobbed. "I can't compete with that."

"Come on; you've seen enough," Jake put his hand on Chad's biceps; Chad yanked himself free.

"You wanna play," he snarled at Felix, "play with *this*." He leaped forward, landed on the bed, drew his hand back, claws glinting in the moonlight.

"Chad!" Jake called, teleporting onto the bed.

Chad slashed downward. Jake grabbed his arm, teleporting them a few feet back, but not before Chad's claws took a shallow slice out of Felix's unprotected back.

Felix screamed and jerked up, rolling over and off the bed, eyes wild and terrified.

"Get the hell off of me," Chad cursed, kicking Jake in the belly.

Felix turned on the bedside light. Panting and bleeding, he reached over his shoulder to touch the shallow cuts and drew his fingers away, covered in red. "You psycho bitch!"

"We don't use that word anymore. It's misogynistic. But, I *am* psycho," Chad snarled. "You should've thought of that before."

"Before what?" Felix shouted.

"You know exactly what, you man-stealing—!"

TROY AND I SHARE A PSYCHIC CONNECTION YOU TWO CAN NEVER HAVE, Felix projected into Chad's mind. Whatever guilt Felix might have had was gone in the heat of the moment. *YOU CAN'T COMPETE WITH THAT.*

"I won't have to." Claws at the ready, Chad launched himself at Felix.

Although it was late at night, Pixie and Raven were still in Pixie's office. They stared at the shiny blue orbs altered by an unsuspecting Mandy during the teachable moment with Raven. Mandy's power had altered the devices on a molecular level into pods capable of containing vast amounts of power. Each pod now held a meteor fragment, programed by Pixie, and supercharged by Blake. Each time he had discharged into a piece of the rock, he had burned more fat. His triple-X pants, shirt, and underwear lay like the police outline of a murder scene on the floor. He'd left wearing sweatpants and a shirt scavenged from the lost and found.

"Everything's falling into place," Pixie said. She tilted a dainty teapot covered in tulips. Steaming water the color of a bruise sluiced into a daffodil cup, filling the room with the smell of hibiscus.

"We're close," Raven said, "but close isn't the finish line."

"Indeed," Pixie agreed, sipping the tea.

"What if he doesn't come?" Raven asked.

Pixie set the cup aside and glanced at her phone. "He's already here."

From beyond the door, they heard Desirée shout, "You can't go in there!"

Pixie smiled as Alejandro phased his way into the room. He wore thrown together short shorts, flip-flops, and a white tank.

"It's late," Pixie snapped, but her lips betrayed the slightest of smiles.

"You said you could help us with our powers," Alejandro said, his eyes bloodshot from crying.

"What seems to be the problem?" Raven asked.

Alejandro rubbed his shapely chest, not sure where to look. He blurted out, "I can't touch my boyfriend."

Pixie and Raven exchanged a knowing glance. He blushed.

"Performance anxiety can be a relationship killer," Pixie said. "Fortunately, you've come to the right place. By the time we're done, you and Felix will be closer than you ever believed possible."

She poured him a cup of tea.

"Really?" Alejandro asked.

"But there's something I need from you first." She picked up one of the shiny blue orbs that contained the programed meteor fragment that had absorbed Blake's energy. "I need you to phase this into my brain."

Back at the gay fraternity, Chad was out for blood. He jumped over Felix's bed, claws ready to strike.

"Let's see how Troy likes you when you ain't so pretty," Chad snapped.

His arm swung, Jake dove at him, and they disappeared off the bed in a swirl of pink, reappearing on the other side of the room.

"Dude!" Felix said. "He's trying to kill me, and you teleport him ten feet away?"

Chad growled and shoved Jake aside.

YOU WANT TO STOP THIS! Felix projected.

"I want to rip your throat out," Chad growled.

WHATEVER YOU THINK IS GOING ON, TROY AND I HAVEN'T DONE ANYTHING TOGETHER.

"Oh yeah?" Chad snapped. "What happened to 'We have a link unlike any other?'"

Chad wasn't the only one in the land of desperationships.

Alejandro stood in Pixie's office, blindly following instructions that made no sense to him.

He stood obediently over Pixie as she lay face down on a massage table.

"That's it," she said. "A little to the left."

Alejandro's hand was phased inside her skull, positioning a strange sphere the size of a marble inside her.

Pixie stared at an e-pad held by Raven under her face, showing Alejandro's hand in her cranium. "There!"

"Now what?" Alejandro asked.

"Now," Pixie replied, "you let go."

Alejandro looked at Raven nervously. Raven nodded.

"You chicas are crazy," he muttered as he released the marble. He drew his fingers back, hugging his hand to his chest.

"Well?" Raven asked.

Pixie furrowed her brow. "I'm not sure, I..." She choked on her words, neck arching and eyes rolling back in their sockets. Her body seized, shaking in a spastic fit. Her skin lit with rainbow circuitry all over her body.

"Pixie!" Raven cried, holding her down.

"Stick that in her mouth!" she ordered Alejandro, jerking her head at a rubber cylinder.

Alejandro grabbed it, but before he could press it to Pixie's lip, her tremors stopped. She pushed Alejandro's hand away and sat up.

"You okay?" Raven asked.

Pixie swiveled her head. She took in the room slowly as if through new eyes —and smiled. "I think it worked."

"You sure?" Raven pressed.

"Let's find out," Pixie replied. Her hand struck like a cobra, grabbing Alejandro by the throat.

He gurgled, eyes wide and fingers clawing futilely at her forearm. He tried to pull free, to *phase* free, and he sputtered in surprise and fear at the crackling blue energy dancing around her fingertips, holding him fast.

"How?" he gasped through his struggled breaths.

"Research, technology, and a gift from space." Pixie turned to Raven. "Ready?"

Raven nodded, and lay face down on the massage table.

"Please," Alejandro begged. "You promised to help me if I helped you."

Pixie picked up another of the metal spheres. Again, Alejandro tried to phase free—to no avail. Pixie pressed the blue metal marble to Raven's skull, and it slowly phased into her. Alejandro stopped struggling, processing. Pixie was able to phase!

"I *will* help you," Pixie assured him. "*We* will help you. But your situation is more intricate than you care to admit. Your telepath boyfriend's subconsciously using his power on you. He's keeping you from touching him because he's having dream sex with Troy Allstar."

Tears grew in Alejandro's eyes.

"That's why you came to us. You knew you couldn't fix *that* on your own," Pixie said. "Gay relationships can be so complicated."

Alejandro flailed futilely.

"We really struggled with this technology," Pixie monologued. "There were so many moving pieces. So tricky creating something that could contain the energy in the meteor shard, like Mandy's shield, but could still be phased, unlike her shield. It was the final piece. Once we figured that out…"

Pixie pulled her hand free of Raven's skull, leaving the metal orb inside of her. Raven's body convulsed, and her skin lit up with rainbow circuitry. The muscled woman sat bolt upright. She stared at her hands, flexing her fingers. She grinned as her nails grew into sharp claws. She gazed into Pixie's eyes. "I can feel you," she said breathlessly. "I can *hear* you—inside my mind."

"We are one, dearest," Pixie spoke in evenly modulated tones, sounding like Siri's lesbian liaison. Rainbow circuitry flashed underneath her skin.

"We are one," Raven replied, her voice taking on a matching robotic edge. She gazed at another flare of rainbow pathways all over her body.

"You are next," they spoke in unison, gazing at Alejandro, still clutched by the diminutive Pixie.

She effortlessly flipped him onto her desk. Raven handed Pixie another of the round metal objects. Rainbow energy sizzled in the circuit-like pathways beneath her skin.

Alejandro screamed in horror. Pixie's e-pad projected an image of his brain. "Please don't do this," he pleaded, watching Pixie phase a metal orb into his skull. He convulsed as it clicked into place.

"We will honor our deal," Pixie and Raven said in synthetic unison. "You will be reunited with Felix more completely than you could ever imagine."

Chapter 20

Chad brushed away his tears.

Why am I such a loser that boys always treat me this way? Chad thought. *Why am I never enough?*

"You're not a loser," Felix said. "Sometimes, things get complicated."

Chad punched through the drywall next to Felix's head. "Do *not* read my thoughts."

"Chad, come on, let's get out of here," Jake said.

Chad hissed at Felix. "This isn't over."

Chad took Jake's hand.

"Did you two have fun in Paris?" Felix asked. "Very romantic, drinking champagne on the Eiffel Tower at sunrise."

"We were there with Gibbie," Chad snapped, "as friends."

"Yeah," Jake said.

"That a fact?" Felix said. "If Gibbie hadn't been there, would you have kissed him, Chad? You keep thinking how you could have, or wait, no, you *like* having Jake chase after you so it's better to keep him thinking that you *might* kiss him."

"That's—" Chad started.

"Bullcrap?" Felix snorted. "Don't lie to a telepath. You have the balls to get in my grill when you're stringing along your ex?"

"You're having sex with my boyfriend!" Chad shouted.

Felix's response caught in his throat. He coughed and sputtered. His eyes lost focus. "Alejandro?" he asked, as if seeing or hearing something Chad and Jake could not. "Alejandro!"

"He left," Chad snapped. "I wonder why."

"Where?!" Felix shouted.

"I don't know," Chad chortled.

Felix grabbed Chad by the shirt. "Where the hell is he?"

"Whatever, drama queen," Chad snorted, easily shoving Felix away.

"Take me home," Chad said to Jake.

"Stop!" Felix shouted, and the word cut like a thousand telepathic daggers into Chad's mind.

He toppled to his knees, gripping his skull. "Ass munch!" Chad shouted, but as angry and surprised as he was, Felix looked more shocked.

"I...I'm sorry." He was dazed as he spoke. "I didn't know I could do that. It's just...Alejandro?" Felix grew panicked. "They've got Alejandro."

Chad eyed Felix warily.

"Listen to me," Felix said. "You can hate me all you want. But this isn't about me or you. Don't punish Alejandro for what I did."

"If this is your way of changing the subject..." Chad warned.

Felix doubled over, grasping his stomach in pain. "They're hurting him. Oh, God, what are they doing to him?"

Felix grabbed Chad's forearm. The older youth's lips trembled. "Soon, we will all be united in love."

"What?" Jake asked.

Felix shook himself back into the moment.

"Raven and Pixie," the telepath explained, "they put something inside Alejandro's skull. They're turning him into one of them."

"What?" Chad said. "That's not a thing."

"Was it a metallic marble?" Jake asked, recalling the tech Pixie showed them.

Chad pinched his nose. "We are such idiots."

"We have to help him!" Felix's eyes wandered, staring at something only he could see. "Oh, hell."

"Where are they?" Chad asked. "The farmhouse? Jake can teleport us there."

"It's too late," Felix said, shaking his head fearfully. "They've left."

"Where are they going?" Jake pressed.

"Here," Felix replied. "They're coming here."

Purple-pink energy flared in the bedroom, and there stood Desirée and Chantal. Alejandro was with them. All of their skin glowed with sub-epidermal rainbow circuitry.

They spoke as one.

"We are here to unite in love."

Chapter 21

"Oh my God, it's four in the morning," Mandy moaned as her phone chirped on her bedside table. She pushed her frilly sleeping mask to her forehead. Her face turned ashen as she read the text message. It relayed a single word.

SASS.

"Shit!" She threw off her blanket, grabbed a pair of jeans, and pulled on a shirt. A loud crash shook the house and threw her to the floor.

"Mandy!" her mom shouted.

Mandy stumbled into the hall as Pixie fired a tranquilizer dart into Mandy's mom's neck.

"Mom!" Mandy shouted. Pixie and Raven stepped over the fallen woman. Bands of rainbow energy followed circuit-like pathways beneath their skin. The multi-hued glow turned neon pink.

"You will join us," they intoned, "in love."

A swirl of pink light enveloped Raven, and she disappeared.

"Oh crap," Mandy swore, raising her forcefield as Raven appeared behind her.

"You are one," Raven said. "We are many. Defiance is fruitless." The woman pressed her hands to Mandy's shield. The bands of circuitry under Raven's skin grew bright blue—as if feeding off the energy of Mandy's field. It flickered and, with a twa-zap, fizzled out.

Mandy turned invisible and ducked into her room. Raven's ears grew pointed like Chad's. She lifted a dart gun and fired. Mandy grunted as the projectile struck. It hovered in seemingly empty air.

Raven teleported and caught Mandy as her form grew visible and collapsed. More swirls of pink energy filled the room, depositing Chantal, Desirée, and Alejandro. Raven pulled a blue marble from her military pants.

"Welcome, Mandy Kim," Raven said.

"Welcome," the others intoned.

Raven slowly phased the marble, implanting it deep within Mandy's brain.

Meanwhile, a swirl of purple-pink energy appeared in the front yard of the Allstar residence as Chad, Jake, and Felix landed in the middle of Mr. Allstar's marigolds. A garden gnome gazed at their panting frames.

"Alejandro," Felix said, tears in his eyes. "We have to go back for him!"

"We will," Jake assured him.

Chad sprang to the second-story window, pulled it open, and crawled into Troy's bedroom.

"Felix?" Troy called out in his sleep. "Felix, where are you?"

"He's on your front lawn jackass," Chad replied, grabbing Troy and tossing him onto the floor.

Troy woke in a confused sputter. "Chad, what are you—"

"First of all, I'm dumping your cheating ass. Second of all, I'm here to save it, but only because you're Gibbie's brother."

Chad waited for denials, for explanations, for Troy to beg for forgiveness. Chad got none of the above. Troy shushed him, as if he were listening to someone else.

"Troy!" Chad snapped. "The lesbians are after us!"

"I know," Troy said, tapping his forehead. "Felix told me."

"Of course, he did," Chad said, nails growing into claws.

Unaware of events unfolding elsewhere, Gibbie at that moment shook an octagonal die and released it onto the board in front of him. He wore a brown dress jacket, plain button-down shirt, and a bow tie, because "bow ties are cool." He tapped a sonic screwdriver against his cheek.

"Tough luck, mister," Blake said with mock sympathy. He moved a blue game piece in the shape of a police call box onto a swirl of cosmic eddies, knocking over a miniature starship Enterprise. They sat in the kitchen of the gay fraternity, the decrepit cupboards lit by candles on the counters. Blake was a fraction of his size of only a few hours ago. Neither of them had a clue they'd arrived at just the right time to completely miss the confrontation that took place on the floor above.

"The Federation of Planets *will* wrest control of the space-time continuum from the Time Lords," Gibbie said.

"You and what Dalek army?" Blake scoffed.

"This one," Gibbie replied, shoving forward a dozen miniature robots.

"They're going to turn on you," Blake warned.

Gibbie shrugged. "You think I haven't noticed the Borg cubes you've got hidden behind your back?"

"Next time, let's incorporate *Battlestar Galactica* too!" Blake grinned.

"Cylons, and Vipers, and Starbuck, oh my!" Gibbie replied.

"You're really cute; you know that?" Blake asked.

Gibbie blushed. "You don't have to say stuff like that."

"Why not? It's true."

"Because I made you feel bad before," Gibbie replied, "and I know what that feels like. And, looking at you now, all skinny and stuff, I hope you didn't do that for me."

"It was a factor," Blake admitted, "but not the only one. The weight gain, it wasn't only from absorbing ambient energy. It made me feel good, so I would do it on purpose, sticking a fork into a socket in secret—but the good feeling never lasted, and I needed more each time."

"You should talk with Mandy. She's been dealing with an eating disorder. This sounds like a superpower version of that. Also, I started reading this," Gibbie said, pulling a bag from his satchel and handing it to Blake.

"*You Have the Right to Remain Fat*," Blake read.

"Whatever you decide is right for you, I support you," Gibbie said, "and I commit to educating myself to become a fativist ally."

"I may have to hold you to that," Blake said, eyeing a power socket. "I don't know if I can realistically stay this thin, and I got the feeling that Raven and Pixie helping me was a one-time thing."

"I am a person of my word," Gibbie replied. "And I dunno; maybe we can trust them."

Gibbie's Daleks surrounded Blake's TARDIS.

"I can't believe you were in Paris only a few hours ago," Blake sighed jealously.

"Weirdness," Gibbie agreed. "Thanks for meeting me so late by the way. I'm too wired to sleep."

"I'm glad you're not too tired to be slaughtered," Blake said, rolling the dice and grinning as he placed five Borg cubes on the board.

"Queer-sistance is futile," Blake winked.

"It is on!" Gibbie said, pressing a button on his phone. He smiled mischievously as it intoned in a robotic voice, "Exterminate, exterminate!"

"So, you had the Eiffel Tower to yourselves?" Blake pressed.

"It was so cool," Gibbie said. "I was there when I called you."

"I'm glad you did," Blake said.

"Me too," Gibbie replied. "And thanks again for picking me up."

"Anytime. We should keep our voices down though. Everyone else must be sleeping. Kind of strange, Pixie sending you to France to help Jake and Chad make peace."

"We also broke into the Louvre," Gibbie shrugged.

"No way!"

"Way," Gibbie shrugged.

"That is so *Mission Impossible,*" Blake said.

"Chad was pretty fierce. But I was the one who had to lift the black rock. Heaviest thing ever."

Blake tilted his head.

"Yeah," Gibbie said, flexing his scrawny arm, "it's impressive, but no biggie. I'm strong and stuff."

"Black rock?" Blake pressed. "Was it metallic? Weirdly shiny?"

"Yeah," Gibbie said, rolling the die. "How'd you know?"

His Daleks took out one of Blake's Borg cubes.

"Huh," Blake grunted, taking the dice from Gibbie's hand. "It's probably nothing; it's just, the way I was able to discharge so much energy was into pieces broken off a chunk of black rock."

"Pixie's doing some experiments, but then we'll return the rest to a First Nation," Gibbie said as Blake's roll knocked out a pair of Daleks.

"You don't think they're playing us, do you?" Blake asked, putting his hand on top of Gibbie's.

They paused at Blake's words, knowing all too well what happened in stories when characters said such things. They tensed, waiting for the earth to shake, the windows to blow in, and for the maniacal laughter of ne'er-do-wells to echo through the halls.

Instead, they were greeted by the sound of hissing candle wax. They laughed nervously. Blake withdrew his hand. In a moment of boldness, Gibbie put his hand on top of Blake's.

Blake swallowed hard. "Whose roll is it?"

"My move," Gibbie replied, and he leaned in for a kiss.

Blake's lips were soft and tender, and Gibbie felt warmth blossoming in his chest, reaching out to fill his whole body. Blake pulled away. They stared into each other's eyes, then kissed once more.

"I really like you Gibbie."

122

"I like you too," Gibbie replied, touching Blake's face.

Their lips moved towards each other like magnets, only to be interrupted by the beep of Gibbie's cell. He would've ignored it, but he could see his phone on the table, and the message in all caps turned his skin ashen.

"What's the matter?" Blake asked.

"We have to move," Gibbie replied. "Now."

"What?" Blake asked. "Was my kiss that bad?"

Gibbie held up the phone.

"It says SASS," Blake read out loud.

"That's our code for get the hell out." Gibbie grabbed his jacket and satchel from the back of the chair. "We came up with it after we found that warning in Troy's Paris Hilton journal."

Gibbie's phone rang. "Troy," he said. "I got the text. Is everything okay?"

Gibbie nodded as Troy spoke.

"I'm at the fraternity with Blake. No one's attacked us. They were here? Blake must've been picking me up; we probably just missed them. They can teleport? Oh, crap."

As if called by Gibbie's words, circles of pink energy erupted around him and Blake, depositing the four lesbians, dressed in leather. Alejandro and Mandy were with them, similarly dressed. Lines of circuitry glowed under their skin.

"We are one," they intoned.

"Mandy?" Gibbie breathed into the phone.

She stepped forward. "You will join us, in love," she said.

They closed in.

Blake grabbed a fork and shoved it into an outlet. His body shuddered and bulged as energy poured into him. His other palm fired red lightning. It hit Raven and Pixie. They staggered back, then straightened, the lines of circuitry under their skin glowing red.

"I think you're making them stronger!" Gibbie squealed, ripping up the floorboard and throwing Mandy off balance.

"You will join us in love," they chimed.

Blake grabbed Gibbie and kissed him. Red energy flowed from Blake to the smaller teenager. "Thanks!" Gibbie said. He slammed his palms together, unleashing a concussive wave that sent the table, chairs, and board game flying. Their enemies were unmoved, phasing to allow the energy and objects to pass through them like ghosts.

"Crap," Blake swore, his hand seeking Gibbie's. Their fingers squeezed together.

Pixie and the others reached for the pair, and a swirl of purple appeared in front of them, leaving Jake in its wake. He grabbed Gibbie and Blake—"later ladies," he said—and teleported away.

Moments earlier, at Nuffim Mall, Troy paced back and forth in front of a table of Aberbombie and Stitch rugby shirts and a giant poster of a muscled brunette in jean shorts. The guy was grinning. Troy was not. He was shirtless and barefoot, wearing only pajama bottoms.

"Gibbie, where are you?" he shouted into his phone.

Jake and Chad stood underneath a wooden canoe shining with varnish. Chad glared at Felix. He was keeping his distance next to a battered deer-crossing sign on the wall.

"The kitchen!" Troy shouted at Jake. "Gibbie's in the kitchen at the gay fraternity!"

"On it!" Jake said, disappearing in a swirl of pink and purple.

He was back an instant later with one hand on Gibbie's shoulder, the other on Blake's. Troy opened his arms to hug his brother.

"No time," Gibbie said, looking at Chad. "They've got Mandy."

"Motherfrakkers!" Chad swore.

"We'll get her back," Troy said, then to Felix, "Alejandro too."

"How?" Chad demanded. "They can do everything we can do, *and* they can convert us into one of them. We don't stand a chance. They're sharing each others' thoughts for crying out loud."

"Sharing each others' thoughts," Troy murmured, looking at Felix. Chad bristled.

"Haven't the two of you done enough of that?" Chad demanded.

"No," Troy said, "we haven't. Felix, can you link all of our minds?"

Felix nodded. "I think so."

"Do it," Troy ordered.

Chapter 22

Soon after, an Aberbombie and Stitch van whipped along a deserted rural highway. Plastered on the side of the vehicle was a shirtless hunk with pouty lips and a petulant look.

Troy drove. Chad sat in the passenger seat next to him, wearing yellow short shorts, shoes, knee-high soccer socks (he'd never played a game of soccer in his life), and matching sweatbands around his forehead and wrists.

He was shirtless "because we're going into battle," and he didn't want to "restrict" his moves. When Troy had pointed out that dark colors would make for better camouflage, Chad replied, "To win, I need to feel fabulous."

Felix, Jake, Gibbie, and Blake sat in the back on top of boxes of tanks and Tees. They, like Troy, were dressed in Aberbombie wear, tight-fitting full-sleeve tops with three buttons down the front, black shorts that reached to mid-thigh, and matching shoes with white stripes.

"We should talk, about us," Troy said to Chad.

"There is no us," Chad countered, adjusting his wristband so it was half-way up his forearm.

Silence shrouded the passengers in the back. Gibbie shook his head at Felix.

"You know what I'm feeling right now," Chad said. It wasn't a question.

"I do," Troy agreed.

"Then you know I'm on the verge of falling apart, and that it's taking everything I've got to hold the pieces together." Tears came to his eyes. "I can't save Mandy feeling this way. So you're going to make it go away. You're going to make the hurt go away. And you're going to make my love for you go away."

"Chad—" Troy began.

"We've got a mission. And we need my head in the game. If I fail, this whole thing falls apart before it gets started. Besides, you want me to fall out of love with you."

"I don't," Troy said.

"But you do, because it's so much easier for you when everyone gets to walk away feeling great. No yelling. No emotional outbursts. No guilt. That's how you like it. Troy Allstar, good guy."

"Chad—" Troy tried again.

"You'll do it," Chad interrupted, "and you'll do it now."

"I didn't cheat on you Chad," Troy insisted. "It was a dream."

"You want to be with him, more than me," Chad said. "I don't need to be an empath to figure that out. I can't fight for you. I wish I could. But I can only take on so many battles, and with Mandy's life at stake, I choose her. Who knows, by the time you're done changing my emotions, maybe I'll be happy for you both. Now do it."

Troy didn't respond, not out loud, but Chad felt his insides shifting, all the hurt and anger and anguish melting away. Chad knew the drill. Troy was good at making everything better; now, he went further. It was as if Chad's breakup with Troy, the betrayal and the rejection, all happened years ago. Troy dove deeper, making Chad feel like this tragic teen tale had happened to someone else, morphing from a first-hand account to a downgraded blurred memory of a tired TV episode written as mid-season filler. Soon, that faded too.

With a flick of a psychic switch, Chad's feelings for Troy winked out. When he looked at Troy at the wheel, it was a bit of a mystery what he'd ever seen in him. More puzzling was Troy's watery eyes.

"There it is," Felix said from the back of the van, and though Chad's spine tensed at the sound of his voice, it wasn't because he was furious at the guy who'd helped ruin his relationship. It was time for battle. Troy wiped his eyes with one hand and turned the van into the lane leading to the farmhouse that was HQ for the Queeroes' nemeses.

"Troy, watch out!" Gibbie shouted.

Alejandro stood in the path in front of them. He wore skintight black leather pants that blended with the night until the headlights fell on him. The youth's muscular upper body was bare and glistened with blue circuitry under his perfect skin.

"Crap!" Troy shouted. He slammed the breaks, but too late.

A blue forcefield appeared around Alejandro; the van smashed into it. The hood crushed inwards, and airbags sprang to life in front of Troy and Chad. Behind them, the rest of the Queeroes flew from their boxes, cursing and yelling.

Chad slashed the airbags. They hissed and deflated. Chad looked ready to fight.

"Stick to the plan," Troy said. "Go!"

Chad growled at Alejandro, sliced himself free of his seatbelt, bounded out the open window, and disappeared into the night. A swirl of pink deposited

Alejandro outside Troy's cracked window. Alejandro yanked the driver's door off, the sound of crunching metal echoing in the night. He flung the door into the field and grabbed Troy, phasing him free of his seatbelt. Troy swung and his fist passed harmlessly through Alejandro's phased face.

"Defiance is fruitless," Alejandro droned. "You will join us in love." He pressed the high-school wrestler against the ground, pulled a metal marble from a pocket in his leather pants and, placed it against Troy's forehead.

"Some help here!" Troy squealed.

Jake materialized next to them with Gibbie and Blake at his side. Gibbie grabbed Alejandro's solid wrist, struggling to hold him fast.

"He's...strong!" Gibbie gasped.

Alejandro's head turned with a mechanical whir towards the freshman. "And this unit can phase." His arm passed through Gibbie's hand.

Under Alejandro's touch, the marble began sliding into Troy's forehead.

ALEJANDRO, STOP! Felix clambered out of the back of the van, striding purposefully towards his boyfriend.

Alejandro faced Felix, the marble half in Troy's head. *ALEJANDRO IS NO MORE,* a chorus of voices slammed into Felix's head. *WE ARE UNITED IN LOVE. DEFIANCE IS FRUITLESS.*

Felix staggered back, grasping his temples.

"I got this," Blake said, pressing his palm to Alejandro's forehead. "Energy powers that thing in your head," Blake said. "I gave it that energy, and I can take it back."

Blake's voice was triumphant, but Alejandro simply smiled. "The orbs are shielded from you."

"He's right," Blake said, his voice hitting a frightened pitch. "The energy, I can't get it!"

"But we can take yours," Alejandro said, his voice a sinister amalgam of human and computer.

Alejandro released Troy, metal marble sliding free of him, and with Chad's speed and agility, Alejandro grabbed Blake's face. Troy struggled under Alejandro's foot. Alejandro's palm glowed red; his torso flashed brighter and brighter with crimson circuitry. Blake's form, enlarged during the battle at the gayternity, trembled and grew thinner as Alejandro absorbed the energy from him.

"Let him go!" Gibbie shouted, swinging his fist at Alejandro. It bounced off Alejandro's blue shield.

"Ow!" Gibbie cursed, shaking his wrist.

"You want to let him go," Troy said, trying to force Alejandro's boot off his chest.

"No, we don't," Alejandro replied.

"It's me you want," Troy said. "I'm the one who hurt you."

"You hurt Alejandro," he replied in a drone that sounded like a layer of synthesized voices stacked one on top of the other. "We are above Alejandro. We can see the forest for the trees, and the trees in the forest. He is emotionally wounded. We are not. We are united in love. We saved him, as we shall save you."

"You're in there Alejandro," Troy said, "I feel you; I feel all of you. You've all been hurt, your hearts broken. Felix loves me. He loves me so much he made it so you can't kiss him, can't caress him, can't hold his hand. He chose *me*."

Anger flared within Alejandro's eyes.

"That's it!" Troy shouted, casting a tight net around the feelings of calm and control that Raven and Pixie were force-feeding the youth, binding them in a corner while injecting the young man with a concoction of rage and hate; it was all bitter and no sweet.

Alejandro shoved Blake away. Blood swelled the prima donna's muscular form, multi-colored circuitry pulsing in his veins. He held the metal marble in one hand; the other clenched. His foot pressed Troy deeper into the dirt.

"I can hear them in there, trying to leash you," Felix said to his jilted boyfriend. TUNE THEM OUT. LISTEN TO ME, HEAR ME AND ONLY ME.

Alejandro gazed at Felix.

THAT'S IT. LOOK AT ME.

"How could you do that to me?" Alejandro said, his voice losing its Siri-Alexxa edge.

"Let your feelings free!" Troy said, face in the dirt.

At the sound of Troy's voice, Alejandro looked at the teen trapped beneath his boot. Despite a whirl of emotions, Alejandro spoke with a terrifying calm. "I am going to kill you."

Chapter 23

Chad sprinted on all fours through the cornfields surrounding the lesbians' compound. The stalks and leaves cut and scratched him, making him wonder if Troy was right about him wearing a shirt.

Come on García, purse first, Chad ordered himself. *Save Mandy.*

Troy had nullified Chad's feelings for him. Now Chad thought about Jake. Chad's stomach churned at the mere thought of Jake holding him tight.

Forget it. I'm done with boys, Chad lied to himself as he broke free of the cornfield, taking two bounds across the lawn then launching himself onto the farmhouse wall. His claws caught on the aged brick. He skittered up, quick and agile as a squirrel. He flipped into an open window feet first and landed squarely in a crouched attack position.

He was in Pixie and Raven's bedroom/office. To his right was the steel door caging Weapon XY. Felix had told them all about him during the group mind-meld. In front of Chad stood Pixie and Raven. Behind them, standing like sentinels, were Mandy, Chantal, and Desirée.

"Hello, Chad," Pixie smirked.

"Target Feline on site," the rest of them said, speaking in unison. "Recalibrating mission parameters. Alert, alert, unit Can't-Touch-This experiencing distress. Initiating emotional dampening algorithm. Full integration of unit requires resolution with target Know-It-All, AKA boyfriend, and target Romeo."

They're talking about Alejandro, Felix, and Troy, Chad realized.

"Warning," Desirée bleeped.

"Warning," Chantal echoed.

"Warning," Mandy agreed. "Unit designation Can't-Touch-This attempting unauthorized extermination of target designation Romeo. Request denied unit Can't-Touch-This, repeat, request denied. Unit Can't-Touch-This motor function disengaged. Unit restrained."

Chad exhaled in relief. *If anyone's going to kill Troy, it's going to be me.* The thought was gone before he realized it was there—almost. He swallowed nervously. *I'm over Troy…right?*

"Warning! Warning!" Mandy intoned. "Unit Can't-Touch-This paralysis override in progress. Unit attempting self-servo extraction. Extraction complete! Extraction complete! Unit has gone rogue! Extermination recommended."

"Denied," Pixie said. "Apprehend rogue unit and reintegrate."

"Processing," Mandy said. Purple circuitry flashed under her skin. "Task accepted."

In a whoosh-whoosh of pulsating energy, she teleported away, followed immediately by two more whooshes, transporting Chantal and Desirée in a pair of fuchsia flurries. That left Raven and Pixie with Chad.

Pixie held forth a metallic blue marble. "Chad García, you will be joined with us in love."

"Hard pass," Chad said.

"Foolish Feline," Pixie and Raven replied, "you'll know better once you are one of us. You'll never be alone again. Never wonder if someone loves you. Never be abandoned, like you are right now."

Chad felt a distant pang for Troy.

"Assessing empathic data stream," they said. "Processing complete. Your emotional reaction to Troy's betrayal has been dulled. But dim can be made bright. Wrong turned right. We have Troy's power. We can smother you in love. Or leave you drooling in distress."

"You leave my mess alone," Chad warned, showing his claws.

"You already feel target Romeo's power wearing off," they intoned. "His effect, like his love for you, is temporary. But we are forever."

Raven teleported, grabbing Chad from behind and tossing him against the metal vault door containing Weapon XY. Chad slammed into it and fell to the ground. She towered over him, gripped him by the scruff of his neck and threw him clear across the room. He was a toy; she was a child having a tantrum. His body smashed into the portrait of Artemis and Pinga, knocking it from its moorings and leaving a cracked outline in the wall before he belly-flopped onto the bed.

"You will join us in love," Raven intoned mechanically, marching towards him. "But first, we will kick your sorry ass."

Raven jumped onto the enormous bed.

"Unit Raven requires closure," she said.

Pixie nodded. "Unit Raven shall be fully integrated after closure is achieved."

"Unit Raven will best Feline one-on-one," they said together. "Unit Raven will prove she is superior to target Feline."

"Yeah, and all you need is a bunch of superpowers to do it," Chad snarled.

"Processing target Feline's use of combative verbal strategy—colloquially known as 'talking smack,'" Pixie and Raven said.

"That wasn't smack," Chad replied. "That was full-on shade."

"Processing complete," Pixie and Raven said. "Target Feline must be defeated in a 'fair fight' for unit Raven to achieve closure. Unit Raven will refrain from use of any powers except for those derived from target Feline."

"Bring it on," Chad replied.

Raven cracked her knuckles, grew long claws, and bared her fangs. They launched towards each other; colliding mid-air, they fell to the mattress in a swirl of slashing claws. Jaws snapped and bit deep as they vied for an advantage. A torn pillow sent up a cloud of bloodied feathers.

They pulled away, snarling, wounds oozing red. They circled and pounced. Chad dove low, grabbed Raven's ankle, and swung her body, smashing her head into the wall. He was on her in a flash, teeth on her neck, ready to rip her jugular to pieces. It was kill or be killed. His jaw snapped shut...on nothing. He looked in surprise at Pixie's arm phased through his chest, grabbing Raven, pulling her through Chad's body and setting her on her feet.

"Cheater," Chad said, backing away.

Pixie wagged her finger. "Target Feline is mistaken. Unit Raven lost. Processing loss. Processing..."

Raven panted, glaring at him, looking anything but satisfied.

"Unit Raven wants a rematch," Raven said.

"Denied," Pixie replied. "Target Feline will now be joined to us. His best traits will inspire new code. His preening vanities will be deleted."

Come on, Jake, Chad thought, sweat pouring down his body. *For once in my life, do not leave me hanging.*

"Prepare for perfection," Pixie said as Raven scowled. "Prepare to join us in love."

Chapter 24

On the path leading to the farmhouse, Alejandro threw Blake aside. Gibbie caught the youth.

"Blake!" Gibbie cried.

Blake was a skeleton held together by skin. His eyes bulged in his skull. "Tired," he wheezed.

"You are a dead man," Alejandro seethed at Troy, grabbing him by the throat and yanking him into the air.

Troy sputtered a laugh. "You can't kill me. They won't let you. I feel them holding you back."

Alejandro struggled to squeeze the life from Troy and found his fingers frozen. "Unit designation Can't-Touch-This attempting unauthorized extermination of target designation Romeo," he droned mechanically. "Request denied unit Can't-Touch-This, repeat, request denied. Unit Can't-Touch-This motor function disengaged. Unit restrained."

"See?" Troy said, grasping Alejandro by the wrist to take some of the pressure off of his neck. "You're their puppet, and once you assimilate me, you're going to be stuck with me and the memory of everything I did with your boyfriend—forever."

"No!" Alejandro growled. With a force of blinding will, he threw Troy to the ground. Alejandro's free hand jerked fitfully upwards as if fighting an unseen force. He grit his teeth, chest heaving, biceps and shoulders clenched as he lifted his hand inch by inch.

"Warning! Warning!" Alejandro intoned like a human PA system. "Unit Can't-Touch-This paralysis override in progress."

"Damn right, it is," he shouted, shoving his fingers inside his own skull.

"Warning! Warning!" he intoned mechanically. "Unit Can't-Touch-This attempting self-servo extraction."

With a satisfied grunt, he yanked out the orb that had been controlling him.

"Extraction complete," he said with an exhausted sigh. He dropped to his knees, panting, his physique a waterfall of sweat. "I'm going to kill you, Troy Allstar," he gasped, "as soon as I catch my breath."

"I'm not your biggest problem right now," Troy said as a trio of pink energy cyclones deposited Mandy, Desirée, and Chantal, rainbow circuitry pulsing under their skin.

"Blake! Jake!" Troy shouted.

Felix helped Alejandro up.

"Do not touch me!" Alejandro snapped, then he realized, "You're touching me! We can touch!"

"I need those," Gibbie said, taking the two marbles from Alejandro's hands. Blake's rake thin form quivered in Gibbie's free arm.

Gibbie squeezed his fist on the pair of orbs; they fractured with a frightening boom. Fissures of red energy pushed through. Blake closed his fingers around them, his entire body trembling as he absorbed their power. His face filled out, and his body ballooned like someone was blowing air into him.

"That's better," Blake said, standing on his own.

"Defiance is fruitless," Mandy and the other two intoned. "You will all join us in love."

The trio surrounded the Queeroes. The women closed in, metal marbles thrust menacingly in front of them.

"This is a lot of people to teleport," Jake said as the Queeroes stood back to back, "*and* I've never been to their HQ before. Your plan better work, Troy."

"You love Chad," the wrestler replied. "Focus on that."

As Mandy and the others stepped closer, the Queeroes joined hands in a circle.

Please lord, let this work, Troy prayed, opening up his power. He felt what Jake felt for Chad. The emotion was like an injured bird, wing broken, huddled inside Jake's protective palms, shielding it from the world.

"Remember the first time you had feelings for Chad," Felix said.

"Guys!" Gibbie said as Mandy held a metal sphere an inch from his forehead.

"That's it," Troy said. He felt Jake's heart open; warmth spread outwards, and the injured bird spreading its wings. Troy's empathic powers added a rush of air, daring it to fly.

Troy felt tears in his eyes as he intensified the feel of Chad's caress, his laugh, his utter devotion. Jake's eyes welled, knowing those feelings all so well. With that, the broken bird took flight, blazing like a rainbow phoenix rising from breakup ashes.

That's how Felix makes me feel, Troy realized.

I KNOW WHAT YOU MEAN.

"We know what you're thinking," Mandy droned. "Your plan will fail."

"And I know what you're thinking, Mandy Kim," Felix replied. "Password, Markham."

Mandy hesitated. Felix cashed in on the distraction, searching for Chad's mind across the field. Felix furrowed his brow.

"What's wrong?" Alejandro asked.

"It's Chad," Felix said. "His thoughts are scattered. I can't get a lock on him!"

"Say my thoughts to your thoughts!" Gibbie shouted, pulling his head back from the metal marble in Chantal's outstretched hand.

"What?" Felix demanded.

"My thoughts to your thoughts!" Blake echoed. "Just do it!"

Desirée pressed a metal orb to Felix's forehead.

"My thoughts to your thoughts," he said, "My thoughts to your thoughts...come on Chad, let me in..."

Felix's gaze widened.

"I've got him!" Felix said, seeing the world through Chad's feline eyes, hearing the world through Chad's ears, and the smells, conveying more information than Felix imagined possible.

He experienced Chad in the farmhouse; he crouched. On one side of him loomed Raven. On the other, Pixie. Raven teleported in a whirlwind of energy, appearing behind Chad. She threw him against the steel door imprisoning Weapon XY.

"You will join us, in love," Raven intoned, marching towards him.

"But first," Pixie said, "we will kick your sorry ass."

"You getting this, Jake?" Felix asked, projecting everything he was reading from Chad's mind into Jake's.

Come on, Jake, for once in my life, do not leave me hanging.

"Got it!" Jake shouted. "Blake! Juice me up!"

Jake squeezed Blake's hand, and the energy Blake absorbed from the orbs flooded into Jake. Jake's body took it and transformed it into swirling purple and pink tendrils.

"I'm coming for you, babe," Jake declared. Pulsating energy exploded from him as he teleported the circle of gays away.

Chapter 25

Raven and Pixie closed in on Chad.

"Jake," he mewled desperately.

A supernova of purple-pink power va-boomed between him and the encroaching women. Jake, Blake, Troy, Felix, Alejandro, and Gibbie landed around him.

Mandy, Desirée, and Chantal bwa-ooshed into a military flank next to Pixie.

"Finally," the women said in unison, rainbow circuitry flaring under their skin, "we can end this."

Pixie held up a metal orb. "Who will be first?"

She let the silence drag—as if someone would volunteer.

"To hell with this," Gibbie said, lifting the massive oak desk…

"*I do not consent to this,*" Muriel admonished.

…and throwing it at Pixie. She phased, and the projectile smashed to bits against the steel door caging Weapon XY. Raven teleported and rematerialized in front of Gibbie, the back of her hand smacking him and sending him flying against the wall.

"We will start with him," the women intoned as Gibbie got up.

"Leave him alone!" Troy said, tackling Raven with all his football and wrestling skill. It was enough to buy a few seconds, but no more.

She threw him aside with the same super strength Gibbie possessed. Desirée caught Troy by the wrist. He dangled in her grip, like a fish on a hook.

Mandy closed in on Chad.

"Come on, Mandy, I know you can hear me," he said, backing away.

"We all hear you." Her ears grew pointed. "You will join us in love."

"Not today," Alejandro said, floating up through the floor, hovering like a ghost behind her. He stuck his hand through the back of her skull, grabbed hold of the marble enslaving her, and yanked it free.

She gasped and fell into Chad's arms. "I'm so sorry," she panted.

"So are we," Pixie said from behind Alejandro. She kicked his feet out from under him. He would've smacked the floor face first, but Pixie grabbed him by the waistband; she jerked him up and slammed him to his knees.

He grunted in pain, mind fumbling to reorient himself. Pixie's claws dug into either side of his head. He screamed. Instinctively, he phased for freedom, but her molecules morphed in tandem, holding him in a tightening vice. "Expungement of rogue unit Can't-Touch-This approved," the women said in concert. "Delete! Delete!"

Pixie gave a sharp jerk of her arms, filling the air with a sickening snap.

"Alejandro!" Felix shouted in horror.

The handsome youth's eyes glazed over, and his body flopped to the floor. The orb he'd extracted from Mandy rolled out of his lifeless hand, coming to rest at Chad's feet. He stared at it, chest heaving. He glared at Pixie. "What happened to making the world a better place?"

"His hate was greater than his love," Pixie and the others replied in surround sound. "You fight so hard, but I hear your thoughts. I feel what you feel. You are all lost. Mandy, so desperate for love, you kiss a boy you loathe then send him to the hospital for it. Chad, dumped by Jake, yet pining for him still."

"Don't listen to her!" Troy shouted, dangling in Desirée's clutches.

"Troy and Felix, hurting those they profess to love, lying about the one most true to your hearts." Pixie picked up the sphere Alejandro plucked from Mandy. "With us, you would love and be loved unconditionally." She extended the marble balanced on her palm towards Chad.

"And if I say no?" Chad asked. "You'll kill me like you killed Alejandro?"

"Resistance is fruitless," Pixie said.

"Resistance is fruitless," the other women echoed.

"Pixie's controlling the others!" Troy hissed. "She's the key!"

"You will join us in love," Pixie said.

"You will join us in love," the other women intoned.

"No," Mandy said. "You tricked me into helping you make those containment thingies. Not okay." She formed a forcefield around her hand and expanded it against the marble in Pixie's palm. "All I have to do is shift the polarity of my shield and…" As if it were a security tag, the orb cracked, and a fissure of red energy glowed like a hot coal. "Not just good for shoplifting."

"Warning, warning," the lesbians intoned, "orb stability compromised."

The fractured marble ka-boomed in Pixie's face.

Fire and ash enveloped the diminutive woman but did not consume her. She sucked it all in as if she were a vacuum, absorbing the force of the explosion just as Blake would have. She grew taller, the pulse in her veins brighter. "We can only make so many of those with the asteroid metal," Pixie said. "You've just wasted one."

"Expungement of rogue unit Concealer recommended," the women droned in their quasi-robotic voices. "Command-line accepted. Delete! Delete!"

"You," Pixie said to Mandy, "will die next."

Across the room, Felix cradled Alejandro's body.

"I'm so sorry, baby," Felix sobbed.

Raven grabbed Felix and pressed him against the wall. "The deleted unit failed to join us in love."

"Pixie's controlling her!" Troy shouted at Felix as Desirée pulled a metallic marble from her pocket. "You don't like being controlled, do you Raven?"

Raven held a metallic orb to Felix's head. She paused.

"Processing query," she said.

Pixie turned from Mandy and Chad. "Unit Raven, complete command-line. Embed target Know-It-All!"

Raven hesitated. Troy sensed Raven's doubt and used his power to fuel it.

"Pixie hasn't told you everything," Felix added. "She's good at hiding things, even from a telepath, even from your network of minds. But she's distracted, and now I see the truth of her plan. Do you, unit Raven? Do you see what she intends to do? What this is *really* about? Read my mind if you can't read hers."

"No!" Pixie shouted. Troy felt her panic. Pixie clenched the metallic orb in her hand and whipped it at Felix. It smashed him in the forehead with the force of a bullet. His head whipped back and then lolled forward.

"Felix!" Troy shouted.

Raven glared at Pixie. "Deletion of unit Know-It-All was *not* approved." She let his corpse fall to the ground. "Unit Pixie is circumventing established consensus protocols." Raven stomped towards her girlfriend. "What else is unit Pixie circumventing?"

Troy stared at Felix in disbelief. "Felix? You killed him!"

Troy's inhuman wail and empathic powers ripped through the woman holding him. Desirée released him, crumpling to the ground.

"Sensory overload! Sensory overload!" she cried.

"Unit Desirée is in distress," Chantal and Raven intoned. "Overload! Overload! System failure imminent! Expunging unit Desirée recommended!" There was a brief pause. "Recommendation accepted."

Desirée gasped, and her head jerked back.

"No!" she shouted, her voice human and no longer in concert with the others. "They're gone, they're all gone. Give them back!" she shrieked, stumbling like a broken zombie. "Please," she sobbed, "don't abandon me!"

Chantal looked at her and replied, "Command request denied."

Desirée growled at Troy, "This is *your* fault!"

Her fist glowed with red energy.

"Oh crap," Troy said.

She fired. The bolt of red energy sped towards Troy, about to incinerate him. The beam froze an inch from his face. Troy's Mattel-inspired hair glistened in the devilish light.

"What the?" Desirée demanded.

"I'm not letting you do that with my power," Blake said. He stood behind her, palm stretched towards her back. "Energy's *my* thing."

He's holding the beam back, Troy realized. Blake was doing more than that. He grunted, and the red bolt reversed course, slamming into Desirée's chest, emerging out her back, and arcing into Blake's commanding hand.

"No!" she shouted, rounding on him.

"Yes," he replied, drawing more and more energy from her.

"Shielding enabled!" she cried. The energy beam Blake was sucking from her cut out like she'd closed a dam.

She fell to her knees, panting. She could teleport away and leave this madness behind. She had the power to start a whole new life or globe-trot for fun. She didn't. Troy felt her exhaustion, her loneliness, her sense of betrayal from being cut off from the others. She was ready for this to be over. He amplified that feeling. "You'll never be one of them," he said.

"I can't live like this," she sobbed. Tears streamed down her cheeks. "Self-destruct initiated. Three…two…" The rainbow circuitry under her skin pulsed faster and faster.

"She's going to blow!" Troy shouted.

The blast should've been blinding and deafening. Instead, light and sound and all the energy from her final moment turned into a vortex. Blake sucked in every last wavelength.

He glowed brighter and grew bigger, bulging with muscles larger than any Venice Beach meathead's.

He's figured out how to store power as something other than fat, Troy realized.

Desirée remained at the epicenter of her self-destruct blast. It and she shrank, her skin turning grey and pulling tight over her skeletal frame as flesh and sinew converted to energy—drained by Blake. Fractures ran through her. Her lips struggled to move, saying one last thing, "I'm sorry."

Her form shattered to dust. The metallic marble that gave her powers fell to the floor and lay there, cracked and impotent.

"Unit Desirée?" Chantal said robotically. Then, sounding all too human, "Desirée! Target Queeroes have deleted life-partner Desirée! Assimilation mission parameters rejected. Integration command-line overwrite complete. Initiating new command code. Delete Queeroes! Delete!"

"Unit Chantal has gone rogue," Pixie intoned, as if reading off a data screen. "Initiating realignment sequence."

"No," Raven said, grabbing her girlfriend's arm.

"Raven!" Pixie shrieked.

"Unit Pixie has hidden subroutines," Raven growled. "Indexing all files. Searching, searching…"

"Alert! Alert!" Pixie said. "Pause search. Unit Chantal disconnected from server! Reconnecting…"

"Denied," Raven seethed. "Sorting file pathways. Indexing, indexing…"

"You could've been with us," Chantal sobbed at the Queeroes. "We were united, in love."

"You killed two of our friends," Jake said. The Queeroes surrounded her.

"This messed-up world could've had peace," Chantal insisted. She fell to her knees in front of the pile of dust that was once Desirée.

"I'm sorry," Blake said. His palm glowed red.

She snorted. "I can shield myself from your power," she said, "and I will kill you all before I self-destruct."

"This," Blake waved his charging fingers, "isn't for you." he touched Chad's back, superpowering him. Chad moved faster than he ever had, a whirl of claws and teeth.

She phased. "I'm untouchable."

"Not exactly," Gibbie replied. He grabbed Mandy, and he threw her at Chantal. Mandy flew straight as an arrow, arm outstretched, fingers squeezed tight. Her fist penetrated Chantal's phased face. Mandy activated her shield around her hand and punched the metallic orb from Chantal's mind. The back of the woman's skull burst in a spray of blood, brains, and bone. The high-tech marble smacked against the wall and thudded on the carpet. Mandy flipped and landed on her feet. A blue shield sizzled around her knuckles.

Chantal gasped and crumbled to the ground.

Chapter 26

Raven pinned Pixie against the wall.

DESIRÉE AND CHANTAL ARE DEAD, Pixie said in her mind. *WE MUST BE UNITED. WE ARE UNITED. WE ARE ONE.*

The Queeroes turned towards them. Raven didn't care. She would not be lied to—not after what her brother had done. That programing superseded all others. The taller woman's eyelids fluttered rapidly.

"I *will* find what you're hiding!" she vowed.

WE ARE ONE, Pixie assured her. *WE HAVE NO SECRETS.*

"Alert, alert," Raven intoned. "Corrupt data detected."

"She's an empath now," Troy said. "Whatever you're telling her, she knows you're full of it." He stared at Felix's dead face. Troy's voice grew to a bellow, "Show her the truth!"

"Show me!" Raven echoed, the combined weight of their empathic projections slamming into Pixie. "Password Caleb!"

"Overload! Overload!" Pixie squealed, squirming in Raven's grasp. "Command abort!"

"Denied," Raven said. "Seeking ghost files. Ghost files detected. Files encrypted. De-encryption initiated. Accessing files."

"Deleting data, deleting data!" Pixie cried.

"Override!" Raven shouted. "Unlocking files. Unlocking files—"

"Fine!" Pixie shouted. "You want the truth, here it is!"

"Data accessed," Raven agreed. Her voice died, eyes flitting wildly as she experienced Pixie's memories in a rush. Tears formed in her eyes, running down her cheeks.

Tears streamed from Pixie's eyes as well.

"You knew," Raven said, pulling back from Pixie and letting her go. "Unit Pixie…You knew it was him."

Pixie wiped the tears from her cheeks and gazed at Raven.

"Not at first," Pixie said. "When Caleb came to me, he looked like you, he sounded like you, he acted like you, he *smelled* like you."

"Yet when he kissed you…" Raven began

"…when he kissed me, something was different."

Troy, Chad, Gibbie, Mandy, Blake, and Jake watched, waiting, unsure what to do.

"You didn't pull away." Raven clenched a fist.

"I wanted to want to," Pixie said.

"But you *didn't* want to," Raven realized.

"I loved your brother," Pixie admitted. "I always loved him."

"More than me," Raven realized.

"Yes," Pixie agreed.

"If he'd been a woman—" Raven began.

"You never would've stood a chance," Pixie finished for her.

"Then he *was* a woman," Raven connected the dots. "Not just any woman. He was me. But he was him too. He was everything you ever wanted."

"When you walked in, and the illusion broke, it was all too much," Pixie said. "I needed time to process. After you locked him up—"

"You couldn't stop thinking about him. All *this*," Raven gestured around, "was so you could have that illusion again."

"On *my* terms, under *my* control," Pixie replied.

"You want to make Caleb one of us," Raven said incredulously. "I gave up everything for you." Raven looked at the multi-colored circuitry glowing under her skin. "I became a *thing* for *us*."

Raven looked deeper, accessing more memories, more thoughts, more files on the hard drive that was Pixie's brain.

"After everything I've sacrificed, after all we've been through, you still love him more than me."

"It won't matter once we're united," Pixie said. "We will all love and be loved. He's your brother. Your family will be whole and healed."

"No," Raven replied. Her fist glowed with a blue forcefield. She swung at Pixie—and froze. She blinked in surprise.

"Unit Raven servo functions disengaged," Pixie explained. "I wanted to do right by you. I owed you that much. But I can't have you ruining this for me. I've sacrificed too much. Goodbye, Raven."

"Pixie, what are you doing?" Raven demanded.

"Unit Raven self-destruct initiated," Pixie said.

"Override!" Raven shouted.

"Access denied," Pixie said.

"You're going to kill your girlfriend?" Mandy demanded. "That is cold."

Raven gazed at Felix and Alejandro, at their bodies on the floor, and then back to Pixie.

"Do you see what you've become? Raven asked. "A cold-blooded killer."

Pixie shook her head. "The Raven I know doesn't get squeamish at the sight of blood."

"And the Pixie I know doesn't revel in it."

"I don't—" Pixie said.

Raven nodded. "But you do. I'm an empath and a telepath. Your thoughts to my thoughts."

"My feelings to your feelings," Pixie added miserably. "Countdown initiated. Three, two…"

Pixie threw her arms around Raven. The explosion was deafening, the heat incinerating Raven down to her last drop of blood, but the violent flare did not go beyond Pixie's arms. She possessed Blake's power to absorb energy, and she sucked every ounce of her exploding lover into herself. A cracked metallic marble dropped to the floor—all that was left of Raven.

Pixie's biceps bulged, and she grew two inches taller; she pulsed with a red glow. Blake still dwarfed her.

"Your turn," she said to him.

"I know how to deal with villains," he replied.

He swung his fist towards her. She caught it in her palm.

"I know all about what you did to the other units," Pixie said, holding him back with the strength of a Gibbie, "and I've learned from their mistakes." Her free hand struck like a cobra, phasing through Blake's chest. She gave a jerk and a twist. Blake grunted. She yanked her hand free, holding his heart.

"No!" Gibbie shouted.

"You took my friends from me," she said to them. "Turned my girlfriend against me. Now, I will take everything from you." Blake's heart sizzled and cooked in her hand, dissolving to ash under a barrage of red sparks. His body fell lifeless to the floor next to Felix and Alejandro.

"Who's nex—" Pixie began.

Gibbie gripped the steel door labeled Weapon XY. He ripped it off its hinges and smashed it into Pixie before she could phase. She flew into the wall, collapsing in a heap.

"Get up!" he shouted at her.

She struggled to her feet, cracked her head from side to side, and wiped the blood from her nose. "Gibbie Allstar," she said, "the noble defender. Coming to the aid of the weak and the meek. Do you want to know how we powered our assimilators? Blake came to us, desperate to lose weight for you. Here, I'll show you his thoughts and an empathic dose of his feelings."

WHY DOESN'T HE LIKE ME? Gibbie heard Blake's voice in his head. WHY AM I SUCH A LOSER? IF GIBBIE COULD SEE THE REAL ME...GOD I HATE MYSELF. WHY CAN'T HE LIKE ME? I'M NOT THAT BAD!

"Body shame, much?" Pixie asked.

"I never meant—" Gibbie began, reeling from Blake's inner voice in his head, filled with doubt, self-loathing, and love, echoing words and feelings Gibbie knew all too well.

"We couldn't have done this without you," Pixie said to him. "Without any of you."

"Don't listen to her," Troy insisted, reaching out with his empathic powers to counteract hers.

"She's right," Gibbie said. "Blake's dead because of me."

"He's dead because she ripped his heart out," Troy shouted at his brother, kneeling beside him and grabbing him by the shoulders. Gibbie didn't hear. Pixie had taken him too deep inside wallowing grief.

She laughed at Troy. "You cheated on your boyfriend, Troy Allstar. That's how we studied your brainwave interaction with Felix, while you two philandered in a dream. And Alejandro, he came to us unable to touch his boyfriend because Felix was so enthralled by you. You think you're heroes? You're blundering children. You don't deserve these powers."

"Screw you," Mandy said. A blue shield sizzled around her fist, and she punched Pixie across the jaw. She wiped the blood from her mouth and grinned. "Heart number two." She phased her hand into Mandy's chest.

"Mandy!" Chad howled.

Mandy flung her arms outward; her shield exploded in an arc, sending Pixie flying into the wall. She landed on all fours and immediately charged Mandy, loping like an animal, sharp claws leaving deep marks in the floor. Chad tackled her. She flung him off. He landed nimbly between her and his best friend.

"The jilted lover," Pixie said, launching herself at him.

Chad knew he didn't stand a chance. Pixie had Gibbie's super strength, could read his mind, phase, teleport, suck him dry of energy...

I'm going to die, he realized, skittering back. She landed and towered over him.

"Yes," she agreed, "you are."

Jake appeared next to Chad in a swirl of pink, wrapping his arms around his ex, and they were gone in a flash. As Jake teleported, so did Pixie. He reappeared five feet away with Chad. She read Jake's mind and was there half-a-heartbeat later.

"There are so many ways I could erase you, but you're a songwriter, so let the punishment fit the Alanis Morissette lyric."

She pressed her palm to Jake's chest. Red energy ran out of her and into him. His body glowed red, the light growing brighter and brighter. He gurgled in pain, eyes rolling back, and in a flash of crimson lightning, he teleported away.

"Isn't it ironic?" Pixie asked of no one.

"What did you do to him?" Chad demanded.

Pixie grinned maliciously. "Overcharged him. He'll teleport over and over until something gives. I'm betting aneurysm."

Jake reappeared, sopping wet and coughing salt water. He fell to one knee, clutching his chest.

"I can't make it stop!" he said.

In a swirl of red lighting, he was gone. Chad's claws swung at Pixie and passed through her. She threw her arms wide; a forcefield blew outwards, sending Chad smashing into a bedpost.

"Two can play at that game," Mandy said, sending her shield at Pixie. Pixie turned, erecting a forcefield of her own. Mandy's field hit Pixie's, creating a concussive blast that sent Mandy one way, Pixie the other. Mandy hit the wall and dropped unconscious.

Pixie's eyes rolled in her head, and her body twitched. "Warning, warning," she intoned mechanically. "Biological systems compromised. Shield inoperable."

Troy grabbed a brick, fallen to the floor from all the fighting, and jumped towards her. She caught his wrist and squeezed. He howled and dropped the makeshift weapon. Chad hurled himself towards her, claws extended, and Jake appeared right in front of Chad, red lighting crackling from Jake's skin. Chad sheathed his claws, smashed into Jake, and the two disappeared in a swirl of red.

"And then there was one," Pixie said, twitches rippling beneath her skin as the rainbow circuitry under her dermis pulsed. "Ready to have your bones broken one by one, Troy Allstar?"

Chapter 27

Jake and Chad rematerialized in the middle of a warehouse club. Electronica music pounded the air, green lasers fired overhead, refracting off a gigantic, twirling disco ball. A drag queen with a towering pink beehive mouthed the words to 'Starships' while half-a-dozen shirtless go go boys gyrated in sync behind her. The pumped posse wore the tiniest of sparkling blue booty shorts and winged limited edition runners. Their queen was bedecked in a quasi-futuristic silver bustier that screamed "send out the femme bots!" They twirled and high-kicked their way through an intricately choreographed routine.

In the middle of the dance floor, Jake clung to Chad, looking like a tweaked-out raver. The former football star's eyes blazed with red energy. Shirtless partiers packed around them, sweating and grinding against one another, cheering on the performance as the drag queen shot streamers into the air.

"Where the hell are we?" Chad yelled over the music.

"Berlin," Jake said, panting and leaning on Chad for support.

Jake's body glowed with swirls of red. He looked about wildly.

"It's too much," Jake whimpered. "I can't hold it!" Pulsing crimson power formed around them, and they were gone.

They reappeared in the diner where Jake used to bring Chad what seemed a lifetime ago. Jake staggered to the freezer, grabbed a tub of ice cream, and spooned Bitter Cherry into his mouth. He dropped the utensil.

"Oh crap," he clutched his heart, leaned against the wall, and lowered himself to the floor. "It hurts so much." Sweat poured from his forehead.

"You're burning up," Chad said. He grabbed a handful of napkins to wipe Jake's glistening form.

Veins crisscrossed Jake's body, throbbing with a scarlet tempest. He hugged his knees to his chest, rocking back and forth. Chad cradled Jake and tried to spoon-feed him. Jake shoved the food away.

"Please, make it stop," he begged as his muscles convulsed. His veins looked ready to split.

Red energy erupted from his every cell, wrapping around him and Chad.

They reappeared in a bowling alley. The lights were out. A neon sign in the window buzzed *CLOSED*. The pins cast silent shadows in the moonlight dappling the front entrance. Chad recognized the place. *Nuffim Strikes*. His dad loved it here.

Sitting in the middle of a bowling lane, Chad held Jake and gazed around desperately for something that might help.

"There are chips," Chad pointed to the food counter, but he didn't dare get up, too afraid Jake would teleport again, and Chad wouldn't be there to help.

"Doesn't matter," Jake shook his head. "I'm not short on energy. I have too much. Not sure how much more my heart can take. I'm sorry, Chad. I'm sorry I dumped you, left you, and treated you like I did. I missed you every day we were apart. I love you, babe. I love you so much."

With that, Jake shoved Chad off of him and teleported away.

"Jake!" Chad said, tears streaming from his eyes. "You get back here right now you piece of sh—!"

Jake reappeared one lane over. He looked about in confusion. Chad jumped at him, but Jake was already gone, rematerializing by the soda machine.

"Stay there," Chad ordered. "I'm coming."

Jake teleported and wound up in front of a set of 10 pins. He could barely stand.

"Jake!" Chad said.

Jake staggered two steps towards his ex, teleported, and reappeared in Chad's arms. Blood trickled from Jake's nose.

"This is where it started," Jake said. "I guess it's fitting this is where it ends."

"This is where what started?" Chad asked.

"This is where I figured out I was gay. At the school bowlathon, I saw you in a pair of tight jeans, your biceps popping the sleeves of a floral T-shirt and your butt doing the same to your stretchy jeans. I had to hide my boner behind a bowling ball."

Pressed together, Chad gripped the top of Jake's pants to hold him up.

"Don't go," Chad begged, his voice catching on the words.

"Not my choice this time," Jake replied.

"Bullshit," Chad said, kissing him deeply.

Jake kissed back, wrapping his meaty arms around Chad one last time. Jake felt the energy building inside of him. He knew he should push Chad away; for once, Jake held on tight and let his feelings go. A swirl of energy erupted from

146

him. It was neither red nor pink nor purple. It was milky white, wrapping a fog around them that exuded a gentle light.

The bowling alley was gone. A glowing cloud engulfed them. They floated in a place where time seemed to have stopped; there was only Jake staring into Chad's eyes and Chad staring into Jake's.

They stayed suspended like that, not speaking, not moving, simply being. Sparkles twinkled around them.

"I think this is the end," Jake said, hand nestling in the crack of Chad's shorts. "Thank you for being with me."

Chapter 28

"Let's start with your pinkie finger," Pixie said.

With the speed of a hunting cat, she bent Troy's little finger the wrong way. A sickening snap filled the air.

He howled in agony, but he wasn't a star athlete for nothing. He took the pain, focused it into an empathic laser beam, and fired.

She grasped her head, staggering back. "Warning, warning, firewall breach! Unit Pixie structural integrity threatened by target Troy malware incursion. Neural network overload imminent."

Her eyes rolled to the back of her head. Troy's breath came in ragged gasps. He dropped to one knee, cradling his injured hand—but he didn't relent. He growled and intensified his attack.

"Pain threshold exceeded. Countermeasures initiated," Pixie intoned. Her head snapped down then up. "Countermeasures successful. Malicious download terminated."

Troy felt a whipping backlash in his mind as she severed the link.

"System diagnostic in progress," she said robotically. Her skin flared with rainbow circuits as she walked towards Troy. "Diagnostic complete. Status: physical integrity within battle parameters."

Troy stumbled a retreat. "I know what's going on beneath all that rage," he said. "I sense guilt. Fear. Self-loathing."

"Processing," she said. "Analysis complete. Rebuttal algorithms engaged. Discharging rebuke. Unit Romeo sounds like an ineffectual *It Gets Better* video."

"*You* sound like a villain," he replied.

She stopped. "Password villain accepted; self-reflective subroutines initiated."

Troy struggled to figure out the rules of the thing she'd put in her brain. Sometimes she sounded human. At others, she was more machine than woman.

"A court and a judge and lawyers should decide your fate," he said, "for the murders you've committed. But like you once said about us, what court can try you? What prison can hold you?"

He stared beyond her, at Weapon XY's cell. Gibbie had ripped away the steel door that sealed him in. Troy saw the canister that contained Raven's brother. His silhouette was visible as he floated in a milky white fluid.

Pixie followed his gaze. "You think if you free him, he can defeat me. I wouldn't bet on it," she said. "He's a wildcard—for now."

"Doesn't matter," Troy said.

He reached out to her with his power.

"Warning," Pixie said, "hostile connection reestablished."

"You've committed great crimes," Troy said, imagining his words as *Matrix* computer code transmitting over a wireless network into the hard drive of Pixie's brain. "Your guilt is there. It's too big to contain. The more you encrypt it, the more it demands to speak."

He pushed harder, ramming up against a wall.

"Access denied," Pixie intoned triumphantly. "Target Romeo termination authorized," she said, teleporting to stand in front of him. She lifted her hand, red energy crackling between her fingertips.

"Raven's dead," he said, "and it's all your fault."

She froze.

"Password Raven accepted," she droned mechanically. "Access granted."

The dam inside him burst. He flooded her mind with swirls of emotional data, grief filled with regret and loneliness, the woman she loved, gone forever —because of her. Pixie's lips trembled. A tear dripped from her eye, rolling down her cheek. But she didn't relent. She grabbed Troy and threw him into the cylinder holding Weapon XY.

"When I decide to deal with those feelings, I'll deal with them, on my terms, not yours," she said. "I'm not some weak-minded galactic trooper to be told 'these are not the droids you're looking for.' I can feel guilt, shame, and heartache in all their strength, and you can turn them into a whirlpool of sorrow, and I will not drown. Do you want to know why?"

"Because," Troy replied, gasping for breath, "you're a villain."

"Because I'm not you," she smiled. "Now, how shall I delete you? I could suck all the energy out of your body, turning you into a husk. I could phase you into the ground, one body part at a time. Maybe, I should empathically go deep inside your mind, shred every hope, dream, and ounce of humanity in you—then gut you with *your* guilt, shame, and fear; make you beg me to kill you, the way you tried to do to me."

She waited for an answer; Troy smiled. She probed his mind and looked down. Milky white fluid ran around her feet, leaking from the container that contained Weapon XY.

"No!" Pixie shouted.

An instant later, the fluid was gone as if it had never been there. She blinked and shook her head. "It was an illusion," she whispered. She glared at Troy. "You've been waking him up."

"He is *pissed*," Troy said.

Pixie pulled a blue marble from her pocket. "He'll understand, once we are one."

"Is that why you can't say his name?" Troy asked skeptically.

She glared; Troy stepped aside as she marched towards the cylinder.

"I can feel you, reaching out for help," she said. "You still think Weapon XY will save you?"

"Read my mind," Troy replied. "He's not who I'm reaching out to."

A swirl of pink energy appeared behind her, leaving Jake and Chad in its wake.

Pixie whipped around, fast as a jungle cat, claws slashing for Jake's throat. Chad blocked her. She phased through him. Red energy crackled in her palm, ready to incinerate the pair.

"Password Caleb," Troy said, unleashing a wave of emotion into the pathways of Pixie's mind.

The young man in the tank thrashed at the sound of his name. Pixie's face contorted. Conflicting feelings churned inside of her.

"Access granted," she said robotically. Her lips trembled. "This won't stop me," she said to Troy. "Purging files, purging files…"

"This doesn't have to stop you," Troy said. "It just has to slow you down."

"Pixie," a young, lithe man said. He stood in front of her, covered in white goo. He touched her cheek.

"Caleb, I can explain everything," Pixie said. An instant later, he was gone—another illusion. "Caleb?" she cried. It was the last thing she ever said. Jake stood near her. He lifted his arms towards her, but without touching her. He teleported, the waves of his power swirling through the back half of Pixie's body. He reappeared a few feet away, taking the rear part of Pixie's body with him. Her backside stood in front of him, guillotined down the plum line. Pixie's front half remained where he'd left it a few feet away, in front of the canister of milky fluid. Both halves shook, rainbow circuitry flaring wildly. The back half crumpled to the carpet. A moment later, the front half followed suit.

Jake's panting filled the air. Mandy shook her head as Chad helped her up. She stared at what was left of Pixie.

"Does this mean we won?" Mandy asked.

Troy stroked his younger brother's head. "Come back to us, Gibbie," he said. Gibbie's eyes opened. He hugged his brother so hard Troy felt his spine crack.

"Sorry," Gibbie said.

The survivors breathed heavily, staring from one to the other to the bodies of their fallen friends and enemies. Troy felt protective shock wrapping around the surviving Queeroes. Troy's hand throbbed. Emotions were passing back and forth between Chad and Jake like crazy. Troy's temples throbbed, struggling to shut them out.

His eyes drifted, from the steel door on the floor with the words Weapon XY stamped on it, to the glass casement the door once hid.

"Guys," Troy said. They all followed his gaze. A large pool of creamy fluid formed on the floor at the base of the container. Was this another illusion? Troy was sure it was not. About a foot of liquid remained inside the receptacle. Otherwise, the chamber was empty.

Weapon XY was gone.

Epilogue

Jake, Chad, Troy, Gibbie, and Mandy stared at the destruction around them.

Troy cradled his injured finger, averting his gaze from Felix and focusing on the glass cylinder that had been Weapon XY's prison.

Chad squeezed Mandy's hand. She curled her body into his, trembling against him. He turned to Jake, eyes asking, *What now?*

Jake shrugged and said, "I don't know."

The sound of his melodic voice was discordant with the tableau mort surrounding them. They all gazed at Troy's back. He stood alone—as if praying to the leaking cylinder for answers.

"Go," Mandy said, giving Chad a nudge.

He went to the guy who'd broken his heart. "I'm glad you're alive," Troy said, and to Jake, "You too. Mandy, Gibbie, you okay?"

"No," Gibbie replied, kneeling next to Blake and closing his eyes. "I'm not."

He began to cry. Mandy crouched and hugged him from behind.

"I don't know if I can bury any more dead," Mandy said.

"We won't have to," Jake said, grabbing a blanket from the bed and placing it over Felix and Alejandro. Gibbie took a sheet and did the same for Blake. "When I was in Iceland," Jake said. "I did a helicopter tour of a volcano. I can go back to give these guys a burial in one of the most amazing places on this planet."

Gibbie stared at Blake's silhouette. "He always wanted a volcanic super lair."

Mandy set and bound Troy's finger then the Queeroes dismantled the farmhouse's tech. Pixie's computer, Muriel, protested, crying, "*What do you think you're doing, Dave?*" as Jake pulled the plug.

"Who's Dave?" Jake asked.

"You haven't seen *2001: A Space Odyssey?*" Gibbie demanded. "How did I have a crush on you?"

"Is it misogynistic that we just pulled the plug on a female AI?" Troy asked.

"I'm the only female to survive this plotline and *that's* what you think is problematic?" Mandy demanded. "Have you even heard of the Smurfette principle? Read an essay, Aberbombie."

They piled Muriel and the rest of the gadgets in Pixie's office. In the basement, they found the remains of the meteor Jake, Gibbie, and Chad stole for Pixie. Gibbie sledgehammered it and swept the pieces into a metal pail. He carried it upstairs, setting it down with everything else that had to disappear.

"You sure about this?" Chad asked Jake.

Jake applied sunscreen and ate a protein bar. He surveyed the covered bodies of their friends and foes, the equipment they couldn't risk falling into anyone's hands, and what was left of the meteor that was at the heart of the technology that almost destroyed them.

"It'll take a few trips," Jake said, "but yeah, I got this."

"Is it okay if I keep this?" Gibbie asked, holding up the oil painting of Artemis and Pinga. "There's something about it that speaks to me."

No one protested. A moment later, Jake disappeared in a swirl of purple and pink, taking the meteor dust and the container that once held Weapon XY. He appeared above an Icelandic volcano, and let the things go. After a few more teleports, all that remained were Felix, Blake, and Alejandro. Jake brought the surviving Queeroes a change of clothes, and they stood around the fallen, dressed in black.

"I'd like to say a few words about Alejandro," Jake started. "Alejandro, you were *such* a cow. But when the time came, you showed me that no one was going to be the boss of you, not your macho dad, not a bunch of childhood bullies, not some new guy scared of being a pledge, and not a cyborg cult." He turned to Chad. He held a tray of sour-tinis. Everyone took one and toasted to Alejandro. "Here's to you," Jake said. "Give God hell. He's got a lot to answer for."

They downed their drinks and looked to Gibbie.

He wiped his bloodshot eyes. "Blake," he began, "you literally gave me strength, you were my first real kiss…"

"But…" Chad began then silenced himself.

"…and you were right to be worried about the robot uprising, even if they were more like cyborgs. I don't get how their technology worked, but that's not what this unnecessarily convoluted story is about. We failed you, and I'm sorry, and…" Gibbie choked on his words, "why'd you have to be such a goddamn hero, you stupid idiot? You were supposed to live long and prosper! You died young and didn't get to achieve all the things you were meant to." Gibbie wiped his eyes and took a calming breath. He placed a statuette of the starship Enterprise on Blake's chest. "You once reminded me of something Captain

Jean-Luc Picard said. 'Inside you is the potential to make yourself better…and that is what it is to be human. To make yourself more than you are.'"

Troy, Gibbie, Chad, and Mandy murmured, "Amen."

"Ameen," Jake added.

They looked at Troy. He struggled to breathe.

"Are you ready to say a few words about Felix?" Chad asked him.

"I can't," Troy sobbed, his shoulders shaking. It was Gibbie who held him tight.

The next day, Chad and Mandy walked through the halls of the Nuffim hospital. Chad wore a pink t-shirt with a deep V and jean shorts rolled up to mid-thigh. Mandy was in a svelte dress and dragged a floating yellow balloon by a string.

"They deserve to be alive," Mandy said about Blake, Alejandro, and Felix. "And their families deserve to know they're dead."

"We can't take the risk," Chad replied.

They stopped outside a room.

"You sure you want to do this?" Chad asked.

"I'm pretty sure I don't," Mandy replied. "Not that we get to do what we want anymore."

Chad kissed her on the cheek. "Good luck."

"After the last few days, this should be easy," she assured herself, smoothing her skirt. She put on a perky Mandy smile and entered the room.

Markham lay in bed, his arm and leg in a cast. He saw Mandy and dropped his spoon, splattering orange Jello onto his chin.

"You!" he said, eyes wide with fear. He grabbed the nurse call button.

"Silly," Mandy tittered nervously, her heels clacking as she hurried forward. She pulled the console from his bruised fingers.

"Nurse!" he shouted. No one answered. "Goddamn this hospital."

Mandy tied the yellow balloon to the bed. He eyed it suspiciously.

"Come to finish the job?" he asked.

"Markham," she gasped with too much shock. "What are you talking about?"

He glared. "I know what you did to me. I don't know how you did it, but I remember everything."

The TV gargled dramatic music as a soap opera played in the background.

"The doctor warned me you were saying all sorts of odd things. You did take quite a hit to the head," she said. "You gave us *such* a scare, falling down those stairs. I hear your father's launching a lawsuit against the school board."

"There weren't any stairs," he snapped. "I was at *your* locker."

"It's a miracle you were able to crawl that far," she agreed. She giggled and touched his good arm. He yanked it away. She tried to assure herself that this wasn't their worst mess. Gibbie was in mourning over Blake, wracked with guilt. Troy and Chad had broken up. Troy barely spoke to anyone. Chad and Jake were back together. She gave them a month, tops—four weeks too long as far as she was concerned.

"What are you, Mandy Kim?" Markham asked.

There were so many possible answers to that question. Freak. Hero. Villain.

"I'm just a girl," she said truthfully, "trying to get by."

"There was an energy field," he said, staring at her as if she might turn on him. "It came out of you, and it threw me like I was nothing."

For a moment, she wanted to tell him everything.

"How the hell is Gibbie so strong?" he demanded. "And Troy and Chad, how did a couple of queers become the town's It Couple?"

Of all the people to figure it out, who knew that it would be Markham? It was almost funny. Mandy reached for words that dissolved in her gut. She'd played this role too many times.

I'm tired, she thought.

"I'm taking you down," Markham said. "You and your freak friends."

That, she would not allow. Mandy's face lost all expression. Her heartbeat grew firm. She leaned on his bed, one hand on either side of his legs, and pushed her face within an inch of his. "I don't know what you think you saw, but I do know this. I've had a couple of *really* bad days. Prom is coming, and graduation. All I want for the rest of my senior year is to enjoy it. So don't you do, or say, anything, that might ruin that. Do you hear me?"

He tried staring her down.

"I said, do you hear me!" she yelled.

She lunged forward, and as she did, she made the outer layer of her face turn invisible, revealing the muscle and sinew beneath her skin, her bulging eyeballs, a hint of her cheekbone, and bloody muscle. She bit at the air a quarter of an inch from his lips, her skull teeth bared. His head smacked the wall as he pulled away in fear. A second later, the horror was masked behind her pretty face. She ruffled his hair playfully. "Good boy." She stood, winked, and strutted like a runway model to the exit.

"Freak!" he shouted.

She flipped him the bird and slammed the door behind her.

Markham watched her go through a haze of tears. He shook, his heart pounding in his ears. He used to be the baddest of badasses at Nuffim High. Now, he was bruised, broken, and blubbering. *How did she do that with her face?*

"I'm losing my goddamn mind." He wiped the watery weakness from his eyes. He pressed the button for his morphine drip, ready to drug himself into oblivion. Nothing happened. He'd used his allotment for the day.

"Mother of Christ," he swore, slamming his finger onto the call button.

No answer. "I need some effing drugs!" he shouted.

Heeled shoes pattered down the hall. The door whined open.

"Finally," he said, expecting square-jawed Samson, a male nurse with the body of an Adonis who seemed to delight in Markham's discomfort ever since the teen used the term queerbait while yelling at a football game on TV.

In Samson's stead was Nurse Pricks. Her name tag was pinned above her stripper-sized breasts, which were practically falling out of the kinkiest nurse uniform in fetish history. The PVC skirt barely covered her privates, and her top was cut into such a deep V, Halloween stores would blush.

"Hello, Markham," she breathed seductively, reminiscent of Marilyn Monroe. As soon as the comparison entered Markham's head, he could've sworn her face shifted, taking on the doomed star's iconic features.

Her blond hair tumbled about her shoulders, framing pearl skin. Her nails, manicured into ruddy weapons of desire, complimented white stiletto boots riding up her thighs.

She should be working a street corner, not changing bedpans, Markham thought.

She placed her hand on his, making him shiver as she slid her fingers along the muscles of his smooth forearm, taking the nurse call button from his grip.

"You need more medicine?" she pouted.

He licked his chapped lips, nodding, not daring to blink.

"I have a special treatment for you," she said. She pulled out a locket tucked between her breasts and popped it open. A shiny black pill fell into her hand. The capsule glowed with rainbow circuitry. "This will change everything."

156

"It looks homeopathic," he said suspiciously, eyes darting from the pill to her breasts.

"It's an enhancement," she replied.

"Like Viagra? I don't need that," he assured her, trying to swagger with his tone the way his busted bod could not.

"I'm sure you don't," she stroked his thigh, leaning in so close he was sure his breath would steam off her cleavage. "You want to know how Gibbie got so strong? How Mandy nearly killed you? How Troy and Chad became the darlings of Nuffim? This," she held up the capsule, "this can do the same for you. Are you ready to take back the power from those queens? Are you ready to be my king?"

She lifted his chin to stare into her eyes. He wordlessly parted his lips. She slid her finger between his cheeks. He groaned as he sucked it for ten delicious seconds. She pulled her finger free; he whimpered for more, like a milking puppy taken from its mother's teat.

"Uh-uh." She waved a finger at him. "First, you need your vitamins, so you can grow big and strong."

She placed the black pill on his tongue. "Don't swallow yet," she said, reaching into a white nursing bag adorned with a big red cross. She pulled forth a bottle of Etienne water.

For a better life, it said.

"You have to drink it down with this," she said, "and nothing will ever be the same again."

Thirsty, he took the bottle, chugging the water and swallowing the pill.

"That's it," she encouraged, "down to the last drop."

His Adam's apple bobbed with every gulp. He tossed the empty bottle aside. The effects were immediate. He clutched at his heart, struggling to breathe.

"W-what's happening?"

She reached into her medic's bag and pulled out her compact. Popping it open, she held the mirror to his face, turning his chin with her free hand. He gazed at the bruise running from the base of his jaw, up his cheek, and over his temple. Before his eyes, the bruising vanished.

He laughed in disbelief, touching his pretty-boy face. "How the hell?"

"There's more," nurse Pricks smiled.

She pulled medical scissors from her bag and cut the cast on his arm.

"But…the doctor said that was going to take six weeks to heal."

Nurse Pricks shook her head and put a finger on Markham's mouth.

"We don't need any silly doctors, now do we?"

She leaned forward, taunting Markham with her breasts; with a 'pull the bandage off quickly' philosophy, she ripped the cast from his arm. He braced himself for pain from the broken bone. None came. Incredulous, he tested his fingers, flexing them into a fist. Disbelief turned to wonder as he bunched his biceps in and out, experimenting with his range of motion.

He smiled at Nurse Pricks.

"How?"

She leaned in close, her lips hovering next to his.

"Science," she said.

He barely heard, kissing her gently. She crawled on top of him. Part of him noticed that her name tag had changed—not that he cared.

It no longer said Nurse Pricks.

It read WEAPON XY.

If you are struggling with an issue, (or know someone who is) including considering or experiencing self-harm, please reach out to the National Suicide Prevention Lifeline at 1-800-273-TALK (8255), www.sprc.org; the National Eating Disorder Association helpline at 1-800-931-2237, NationalEatingDisorders.org, or the helpline you feel is most appropriate for you.

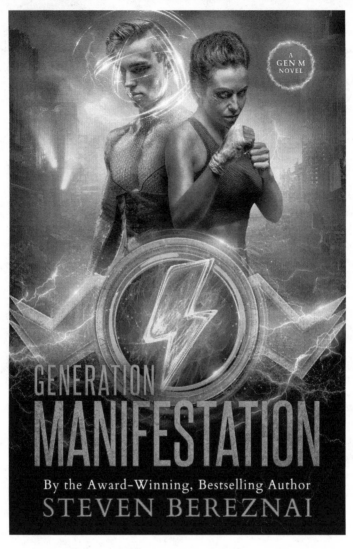

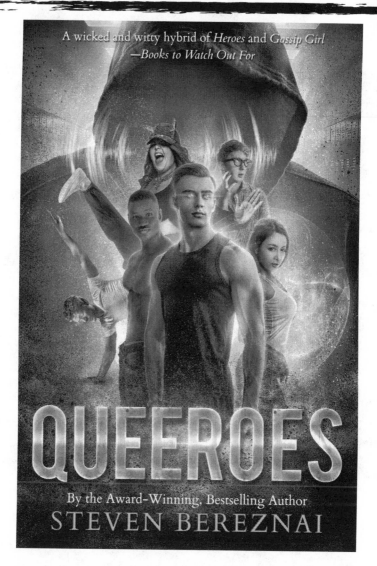

you enjoyed **this book**, please take a moment to write a review on your favorite retailer site and **GOODREADS.COM**. This makes a big difference in selling copies, which allows the author to spend less time at his day job and more time on writing a new novel for your reading pleasure. Shares on social media are also greatly appreciated.

For a free gift, updates on the author's forthcoming projects, digital comics, and curated geekery, join his email list at www.Queeroes.ca. You can also follow his penchant for bent superheroes on Instagram @Queeroes_Gay_Superheroes and other geeky imagery @GenerationManifestation.

Also by Steven Bereznai:

Queeroes

Generation Manifestation (A Gen M Novel)

How A Loser Like Me Survived the Zombie Apocalypse

The Adventures of Philippe and the Outside World

The Adventures of Philippe and the Swirling Vortex

The Adventures of Philippe and the Hailstorm

The Adventures of Philippe and the Big Cever?—

10 Things Every Gay Guy Looking for Love (and Not Finding It) Needs to Know

Author's Bio:

In grade two, I wrote a not-so-breathtaking poem for my school's literary anthology. I've been a writer ever since. My experience includes writing/producing for CBC TV, a short film and reality stint at OUTtv, and penning some award-winning, bestselling novels.

I came out in my late teens and feeling like an outsider has deeply impacted my sensibility. I love writing that combines sass, heart, speculative fiction, and (where appropriate) abs. Basically, shows like *Buffy, Teen Wolf* and *She-Ra and the Princesses of Power*.

I'm Toronto-based and can be reached through my website www.stevenbereznai.com.